a side he'd

Never Seen

A Side He'd Never Seen

Kristie Leigh

Edited by
WALLFLOWER EDITS

Illustrated by
VANILLA LILY DESIGNS

Prologue

Vanilla Girl

In our vanilla world, we'd never done anything like this before, the excitement of having others around heightened the sensations and increased my arousal.

I looked up and caught Alex's stare as he kissed his way down Jenna's neck. His eyes were heavy-lidded, but he kept his gaze on me as James breached the edge of my bathing suit and began circling my clit. My head fell back against James's shoulder, and my mouth dropped open on a silent *oh* as I tried to keep my pleasure quiet. The corner of Alex's mouth curled up as he continued his ministrations.

The realization that someone was watching

me made me feel naughty and turned the intensity up a few levels.

Chapter One

An Invitation to What?

"Have a great day, babe." My husband, James, kissed me on the forehead as he said goodbye while I laid in bed. It was the same morning routine we'd had for the last six years. Every weekday morning was exactly the same, including the spot he planted his lips.

I didn't have to get the kids up for an hour or so, but I liked to start my day early and have a little "me" time before they got up.

"I love you." He smiled down at me, and I wondered how I'd gotten so lucky.

He turned to walk away but stopped. "Oh, Clarissa, don't forget my parents are coming over for dinner tonight."

I rolled my eyes—like I would forget anything. My trusty planner never let me down. "I'll be here; I love you, too."

He kissed me again before he left for work.

It was Monday morning, and I was feeling a little lazy. My outfit waited for me on the dresser —a pair of leggings and a baggy, off-the-shoulder sweatshirt. After brushing my teeth and throwing my hair up into a messy bun, I went downstairs to get some coffee and to check my social media. I still had a few minutes before I had to start breakfast. I tried to cook a hot meal for the kids most days, but today would be quick with scrambled eggs and toast. I wasn't in the mood to go all out.

Two hours later, Lucas had left on the bus to pre-kindergarten, and Jane was playing with her toys in the playroom. I was on coffee cup number three just as my best friend, Amy, walked in with her daughter, Mary.

"Hey, you. Want a cup?" I kissed both her cheeks and poured her a mug, not waiting for her response.

Mary had already run into the playroom without so much as a glance my way.

Amy and I had been friends since our freshman year. Our daughters were born just months apart—which definitely worked to our advantage—and she had moved into our subdivision just after the kids were born. We got the girls together as often as possible and drank coffee while gossiping and binge-watching our favorite sitcoms. Everyone had raved about *This is Us,* and I'd been avoiding it. Who wants to cry through *every* episode? But Amy had finally convinced me.

"Are you ready for this?" She gave me the side-eye as she queued up the show, knowing full-well that I wasn't.

I didn't respond, just sipped my coffee and sat down beside her on the couch. When she wasn't looking, I grabbed a throw pillow to hold onto for support.

"I can't believe we're just now watching this. There are already three seasons out. Better late than never, I guess." She pressed play, and so it began.

Four episodes in and we were hooked, I had cried like a baby, but it was so worth it. We would've kept going but had to stop to make the girls lunch.

My phone dinged with a text in the other room just as the girls went back to playing. Amy plopped down onto the sofa and pulled up her phone before bursting out laughing. There were tears in her eyes.

"What are you cackling at over there?"

"Oh my God. Wait 'til you hear this, Riss." She could barely breathe, let alone talk. "Lisa is having a *Chaste Affair* party."

"A what?" I had no idea what she was going on about.

Amy stopped her fit of giggles and stared at me like I was crazy. "Holy shit, you've never heard of them?"

"Clearly not, what is it?"

"Oh, this is going to be so much fun." She rubbed her hands together. "It's a toy party." She smiled mischievously.

"Toys? Why is it called *Chaste Affair* then?" I was beyond confused.

"Your inner blonde is showing, Clarissa."

It hit me, and I was sure my face went twenty shades of red. "No way. You don't mean *those* sorts of toys, do you?"

That Cheshire Cat grin returned to her lips. "Yes! It's going to be a blast."

"I'm not going to one of those." I shook my head and dismissed the idea. "I have a husband.

What do I need that garbage for?" Single women who weren't in committed relationships used toys. I had the real thing.

When I looked up, the disbelief on her face caught me off guard. I stood there, staring at my best friend, wondering what I'd said that left her mouth hanging open and stolen her ability to blink.

"You don't have *any* toys?"

"Of course not, I've been married since I was twenty-two. What would I have needed one for?"

She finally snapped back to reality and started her inquisition. "Wow! I'm a little surprised. We've been friends for over ten years. How have we never had this conversation? So, you don't take advantage of days like today at all?" Amy stared at me, waiting for a response, but I didn't have one. "You're home alone. When Jane goes down for a nap, you don't get yourself off?" Her eyes went wide when I shook my head. "Wait! You and James don't use toys *at all*?"

I couldn't tell which one of us had lost our minds, but I was hedging my bets on Amy. "Of course not, why would we need to? We have the correct parts for what we do." I wondered if maybe her husband wasn't getting things done and that was why she needed them. "Why would we need other things to get the job done?"

"Clarissa, we're talking about sex, not a *job*. It should be fun and new and exciting, not the same old get on top and let's do this."

She must've noticed my expression of disbelief before I could set my poker face.

Her face scrunched up like she felt sorry for me. "Oh, hunny." *Was that pity I heard?*

"What? There's nothing wrong with my sex life. We have sex regularly." I certainly had no complaints, and James hadn't, either.

She eyed me skeptically. "What do you mean by *regularly*?"

"Every Sunday."

"I'm sorry, did you just say that you have a specific day set to be intimate? Why not just have it when you want it?"

My brow furrowed, and I looked at her in utter confusion—she should understand this. "We have two kids and busy schedules. This works best for us. We know when to be available for each other."

Amy rolled her eyes, and I'd swear she *tsked* at me. "That had to be your idea. Please tell me it's not written in your day planner."

Throwing my head back, I covered my face, completely mortified. She was right, and now that she'd said it, I'd realized how ridiculous it sounded. *I scheduled sex. On my day planner. Every week.* I even had a "sexy" sticker on the top right corner of each and every Sunday.

"Girl!"

I held up my hands in surrender, and I felt my face blazing with embarrassment. "Don't say it. I realize how weird that sounds. Ugh." I sank back into the sofa. "We're happy, though. No complaints from me." I glanced over at Amy, whose brow was arched. "James has never grumbled. Should I be worried?"

"No, no. I'm sure everything is fine, it's just..." She paused and turned to face me cross-legged. "Is it exciting? Are you turned on? Or is it the same thing each time?"

I didn't have to think about my answer, although now that she'd brought it to my attention, I wondered if my answer should be different. "I enjoy it while we're in the moment. It's not *exciting* like when we were dating, but isn't that normal? We're *married*."

"Just because you got hitched doesn't mean you can't have an adventurous sex life." She crossed her arms, and I knew she was getting settled to give me an explanation for what I should be doing. "Stephen and I have so much fun in the bedroom. There's no reason why you can't, too. We mix things up: role play, use toys, all kinds of things. And *no schedule*. Sometimes we do it twice a week, sometimes four, and then there are days where it's more than once a day. We just go with the flow. No pressure."

James and I hadn't had that kind of stamina since we dated, and if I were honest with myself, maybe never. "Sometimes more than once a *day*? Wow!"

"Listen, just come to the party. If nothing else, it'll be a blast. It's been a while since we've had a girls' night. We'll have drinks and stumble home afterward."

I wasn't quite sold. "What can I expect at this thing?"

"Food, drinks, games, and the rep will show us all her products and how they work. After the party, she takes each person into a private room. If they want to order, they do. You can take some items with you if she has them in stock or they ship them. No one knows what you order—

unless you share—and there's no pressure to buy. You can even win prizes."

I needed to commit before I chickened out. "Okay, I'm in." I didn't have anything to lose. It would be fun if nothing else. "I can handle this, and you're right; it's been way too long since we've had a girls' night. When is it? I'll add it to my planner and chat with James."

Her face lit up like she'd won the lottery. "Yay!" She clapped excitedly. "We're going to have so much fun. It's next Saturday at seven."

As soon as Amy had my commitment and had watched me write the date and time in pen on my planner, she gathered her daughter and raced out the door. It was like she was afraid I'd change my mind if she stuck around. The fact that the party was in pen and not pencil meant it set in stone—she should know that.

Amy had opened a can of worms. After she'd left, I couldn't stop thinking about what she'd said. She hadn't even said that much, but it was enough to get my mind churning. I wasn't unhappy in my marriage or sex life. Actually, things were great. Having a routine worked for us.

Or did it?

Now I was questioning it all. Would James keep something like that from me? Was he bored in what we had? Maybe I just *thought* our arrangement worked for us both.

I stewed the rest of the afternoon while making dinner, wondering how I would figure this out without bringing too much attention to the subject. If James wasn't unhappy, I didn't want to plant the seed in him that Amy had in me. But if he wanted more, then I needed to step up my game. And by the time my in-laws had come over, I'd worked myself into a mental frenzy that I tried unsuccessfully to hid. I was sure my in-laws could tell something was off. I wasn't acting like myself, but I attempted to cover it up with a headache.

"Baby, are you all right?" The concern in James's voice made me pause.

I didn't want to lie to him, but I wasn't sure how to broach the subject, either. We were open about a lot of things, but sex wasn't something we talked about often, if at all. I didn't want to give him the wrong impression.

"Yeah, I just have a headache, and I'm a little

tired. Mondays." I shrugged. "You know how it is." I smiled weakly and went back to washing the dishes, hoping he'd let it drop.

Large hands wrapped around me from behind. His breath at my ear caused goose bumps to roll up my spine. I leaned back my head slightly onto his shoulder, feeling a little excited. Damn Amy and her suggestive sex crap. Sundays had worked for years, and now, it was Monday, and I'd done nothing other than think about my physical relationship.

James pressed his cheek to the back of my head and whispered into my ear. "Why don't you go take a bath? I'll finish up here and get the kids ready for bed."

"Are you sure? I don't mind. My headache isn't that bad." I felt horrible for lying and even worse for James picking up my slack around the house when he'd worked all day.

He kissed my neck lightly and then steered me out of the way. "Of course."

"Thank you." I did as he suggested and went to soak in the tub. I couldn't stop thinking about the way I'd felt when he touched me. James was an affectionate man; that was nothing new, but it was like I saw things from a different perspective. My reaction to lean back into him was instantaneous and a tad bit thrilling.

Was that what Amy had meant?

Chapter Two

Where Have I Been?

"What do you wear to this kind of thing?" I stood in my closet in my bra and panties while my best friend laid on my bed, laughing at me. "What the hell are you cackling at over there?"

"You need to calm down, Riss. Dress casual. We're just going to Lisa's for drinks." She was right; it was just down the street. "There's no dress code. Why are you so strung out? You act like we're going to a BDSM club or something."

I whipped around to gawk at her. "A what club?"

Her relaxed demeanor got me even more worked up.

She giggled. "Wow! I knew you were a prude

but had no idea it was this bad. Have you not read *Fifty Shades of Grey?*"

"No." I honestly didn't even know what that was. "You know I don't have time to read." I was starting to wonder what Amy did that she had all this extra time for sex and novels while I struggled to keep up with Sunday romps and daily life.

"Well, make time for that one—or all three. It's a trilogy. I bought it for you months ago." She stared at me, probably wondering what I'd done with the book that I didn't even remember receiving. "You need to open your mind and see what's out there. I know you were young when you got together with James, but damn."

Turning back around, I muttered, "I'm truly starting to rethink our friendship."

"Shut it. You love me, and you'll thank me if you read those books. Dust off the paperbacks I bought you—if you can find them—and promise me you'll read them while Jane's napping."

Rolling my eyes, I reluctantly agreed. What harm could it do? I made a mental note to find the stupid books, and then went back to my outfit selection. Opting for black jeans and a long, flowy shirt with ballet flats, I was as ready as I ever would be.

"Hey, you never did tell me how James reacted to you going to a sex toy party. What did he say?" Amy rolled off my bed and straightened her shirt as we walked out of my bedroom.

"Not much really, I think he thought it was ridiculous." I shrugged.

He was rather quiet about the entire thing. Although he was a little shocked that I was going, he didn't question me.

She smirked, and I didn't miss the mischievous look in her eyes. "He was probably beaming inside, hoping you'd bring home some goodies. But I bet he knows that Little Miss Sunday Sex won't do that." She laughed uncontrollably as she went down the stair.

I knew she was just messing with me, but I couldn't help but question whether she was right.

She must have seen the hurt in my eyes when she glanced back at me. Amy stopped, turned, and took me by the shoulders and forced me to look at her. "Hey, I'm just joking around, Clarissa; lighten up. It's girls' night. We're going to get drunk and have a good time with our friends. That's it."

That's it.

I was going to go to that party with an open mind, and I would stop acting like a stick in the mud. I was too young to be stuck in a rut, and tonight would help drag me out, even if it were kicking and screaming. We were going to have an awesome time. I was determined to have fun and live outside of my comfort zone.

I texted James to let him know we were heading out. He told me to enjoy myself, and he'd be home soon from dinner with the kids. Since we planned to drink and Lisa lived a couple streets over, we'd decided to walk to the party.

From the looks of all the cars in the driveway, we were probably the last to have arrived. And when we walked in the front door, the blush that crept up my neck and onto my cheeks was completely embarrassing. We were greeted right away by our friends, who all giggled like schoolgirls as they put penis tiaras on our heads. The color of my usually pale skin was probably now a deep red, and the flush I felt only deepened as we got farther into the house. It didn't take long to realize that every bit of decor had a penis on it:

the straws, the cupcakes, the balloons. *Every. Single. Thing.*

Amy took in my state of shock and snorted.

"Don't laugh at me, why are there penis decorations all over. I mean, there are even straws shaped like them." I tried to whisper as best I could over all the chatter, but I was mortified by what I saw.

Amy quickly averted her eyes from the corner of the room. Naturally, I looked in that direction and nearly choked on the drink that I had been handed.

I whipped my head back to her. "What the hell is that?"

She doubled over, unable to breathe.

"What is it? That looks like an inflatable man, Amy. Why is that there?" My voice came out with a squeak, I was on the verge of a panic attack. It became increasingly hard to breathe. My chest got tight as I stared at the *naked* rubber dude in the corner, who was anatomically correct —and I dared say, well endowed.

She held on to the counter and took a few deep breaths to calm herself. "That's a blow-up doll." She must've noticed that I wasn't clued in, so she continued, "It's an inflatable male doll with a three-dimensional penis. Some women use them for sexual pleasure; in this case, I promise, it's just a novelty."

I smacked her on the shoulder. She was having way too much fun with my naiveté. I felt like I'd been living in the dark my entire adult life. How could I be twenty-eight and have never heard of any of these types of things? I wondered what else I might be in for tonight.

"Shots! Shots! Shots!" Diana carried a large tray of tiny glasses, shaped like penises.

I wasn't certain that liquor was such a great idea, but I needed something to help calm my anxiety. All I could do was take a deep breath, grab a shot, and go with the flow. Apparently, tonight was going to be a huge eye-opener for me. I just hoped I didn't make a fool of myself in the process.

"Good evening, ladies. I'm your Chaste Affair host for the night, and it looks like everyone has arrived. If you wouldn't mind topping off your drinks and then taking a seat in the living room, so we can get the presentation started. Then we will be onto the afterparty."

The rep was a petite brunette who looked to be in her mid to late sixties. Her hair was slicked into a high bun. She wore dark, smoky eye makeup with red lipstick. Dressed in a sexy, little corset and leather-looking tights, she looked smoking hot for her age. She commanded the room, almost like a strict teacher with her classroom. And I wondered how the elderly could have more game than I did in my twenties, but I could tell this lady had it going on, and I needed to listen closely.

She introduced herself as Bisexual Betty, and I nearly spit out my drink as I choked slightly. BB —as I decided to refer to her in my head—then asked us all to come up with a sexy name for ourselves using a word that started with the first letter of our name. Some were much tamer than others, from Deviant Diana and Kinky Krystal to Wet Dream Winnie. The ones that shocked me the most were Swinging Sara and Anal-loving Amy. I was dumbfounded, to say the least. When it came to me, I said the first thing that came to mind, Coming Clarissa. Amy snickered beside me, but I chose to ignore her.

By this point, I believed I was ready for just about anything, but boy was I dead wrong. I was too embarrassed to ask questions, but God knows I had a ton of them. BB had given us cards listing all the products so we could make notes during her presentation. I marked my card up so much that most people wouldn't be able to read it. I needed to look them up later; I was dying to know more.

BB showed us lingerie, including items like the one she was wearing. I tried to picture myself in them and whether James would like something like that, but it was so foreign that I thought I'd look stupid and he'd laugh.

We also played a few games, none of which I won. Well, that wasn't true. There was a game about sexual adventures. Of course, I had the least, so I won—although I was fairly certain that meant I'd lost—and BB told me I would get to pick a prize later. I wasn't sure what we were playing for, but I hoped it wasn't the man in the corner whose eyes seemed to follow me around the room.

I was in the middle of making a note when the group started to chant my name. I looked around, clueless as to what was going on. Amy stood and pulled me to my feet. There I stood, in the middle of the room, eyes darting all over the place, wondering what was happening. Bisexual Betty steered me away from the group and instructed me to bend over a chair placed in the center of the room.

"I'm going to start slow and soft and then increase the intensity, okay?" she asked me from behind.

I nodded, although I wasn't sure what I agreed to. However, I was too nervous to speak up to ask for clarification. I couldn't see anyone's face but could hear the snickers and comments about needing to get *one of those*. All of a sudden, there was a light tap on my bottom, instinctively I moved to stand and covered my butt.

"Oh, hunny, bend back over; you can handle more than that."

I chanced a glance over my shoulder at her. She was holding what looked like a ping pong paddle in her hand. I didn't want to wimp out, so I did as I was told. It hadn't hurt; I just hadn't expected it or the hint of a sting that followed. The next time I was prepared, so I stayed where I was when the paddle hit my butt.

"How was that, Coming Clarissa?"

I wasn't sure how I felt about this. "Umm, all right." I'd never been spanked or hit in any way before, and making it sexual didn't seem like it should be right.

"I take it from your reaction that you've never been paddled before. Let's see what you can handle."

I gripped the chair a little harder, anticipating pain, but as she picked up the intensity, I got wet. I was mortified by the fact that this had turned me on and in front of a room full of people no less. I tried to keep my face from showing what I felt between my legs, but nothing got passed Bisexual Betty.

"Well, let's give it up for Coming Clarissa." She took my hand and stood me up. "I'm impressed; you took that like a champ."

"Me too. Wow, Riss." Amy beamed, looking almost proud.

I sat back down, my head reeling from all these new feelings. I was kind of excited but in a way I didn't feel like I should be—almost dirty.

"So, the last thing I'm going to show you is a great gift. And with Valentine's Day just around the corner, I would seriously consider picking this one up. You'll save forty-five percent by buying the set, and it will arrive at your door by the tenth. Just in time for the special day."

Betty pulled out a big black box with fancy gold letters on the top and placed it on the table in front of us. I was mesmerized when she opened the lid. Shiny gold and matte-black toys. I wasn't sure what most of the items were. She'd shown us a few things tonight that were similar, and some I could guess on but others, I waited with bated breath for her explanation.

"Now this *Naughty Weekend Away* package has a little bit of everything from cock rings to vibrators to lube. You'll receive eleven toys total and won't have any problems spicing things up this Valentine's Day. I'm sure most of you know what all these do, but let me demonstrate just in case."

One by one, she pulled them out, and I listened intently to every word. BB explained what they did and used a dildo to show us the details and possible positions. When she got to what she called a *vibrating cock ring,* I was amazed.

"So that's what it does? I've been waiting for you to explain that one." I looked up at everyone's shocked faces looking back at me. "Did I say that out loud?" I wanted to close my eyes and tap my heels together so I could teleport back home where I hadn't just stuck my foot in my mouth.

They all burst out laughing, and thank God,

because I was way past the point of blushing and on to complete and utter mortification.

The presentation concluded, and I needed another shot or five, along with more drinks—and possibly and Ativan—so I took it upon myself to make some—drinks, not pills.

"So...what did you think?" Amy popped up beside me.

I eyed her. "Well, I have questions. Like for starters, *Anal-Loving Amy?*"

"Yeah, about that." She shrugged like it was no big deal. "What can I say? I enjoy it."

I had never in my life tried that, and I couldn't imagine anyone wanted to put anything *up* there. I guess it wasn't a big deal, but for someone as sheltered as me, I was in utter disbelief—and maybe a tad bit afraid to admit my curiosity. We'd been best friends since we were teenagers, and Amy had managed to keep this side of herself a complete secret.

I felt like I'd been kept in the dark. "I can't believe we've never talked about this kind of thing before. Isn't that part of the girl code or something?"

"Riss, you've always been a little on the conservative side. I just assumed we were diverse in that aspect of our lives. I now realize we're polar opposites."

"Is there something wrong with me?" My voice came out in a whisper.

"Of course not. Why would you think that?" She reached out and touched my arm, looking at me like she was afraid I might have a meltdown right there. "Whatever works for you guys is your business. But, if you want to spice things up a little, there's nothing wrong with that, either." Amy gave me a meek smile that was intended to set my mind at ease, although with all the alcohol running through me and all the penises surrounding me, I wasn't sure that was possible. "It's never a bad thing to want a little kink in your bedroom." Then she waggled her brows, and I let out a boisterous laugh that caused people to turn our way. "I just happen to be a freak in the sheets." She flipped her hair, and I couldn't help but roll my eyes.

"I'm starting to see things in a whole new light, that's for sure." It might be the alcohol talking, but it was more likely that it was reality smacking me upside the head.

We clinked our glasses, but nothing more was said on the subject. The girls were being called into the den one by one to place their orders, and I was hoping to stay far away so that I could be one of the last to go.

"So, what's everyone ordering?" Leave it to Krystal to stick her nose into everyone's business. *Surprise, surprise.*

I couldn't believe that everyone was so forth-coming with what they planned to get. I must have been in the minority thinking this was private, so I stayed quiet, hoping nobody would notice.

"Riss, do you know what you're buying?" Freaking Krystal.

I wanted to roll my eyes at her need to know everything and smack her for calling me out. I swallowed hard and took a sip of my drink, trying to come up with something to say.

BB opened the French doors just in time. "Coming Clarissa, you're up."

I wanted to kiss this woman, saved by BB. The moment she closed the doors behind us, the butterflies in my stomach made me realize I was more excited than nervous. *Was I really going to order something?*

The room was full of Rubbermaid containers overflowing with products. I'd never seen so many dildos, vibrators, and other pieces of rubber that I couldn't identify in my life.

Betty gestured toward the chair. "Have a seat, doll. I noticed you were a little red-faced throughout the night, and you wrote down quite a bit on your order sheet."

I looked up in shock, I didn't think that anyone had been paying attention, never mind the one giving the presentation.

"Don't look so surprised, I've been doing this for a long time. There's nothing to be embarrassed about. She patted my knee and gave me a warm smile. "We all started out vanilla, sweetie. In this room, there's no judgment. I'm happy to answer any question you might have or give you a little more information on how things work."

I swallowed hard; I wasn't about to pour my heart out to this stranger, but maybe she could answer a few questions for me. I took a deep breath and prepared myself. "I...I'm not sure what vanilla means, but I assume plain." I shook my head, trying to clear away the doubt and act like a grown-ass woman. "I've never used any of the products you showed tonight, but it was informative, to say the least. I think I would like to order a couple things."

"That's great, hunny. But before we get to that, let's get your prize out of the way. You get to choose between a butt plug, mini vibe, or some edible body oil. If you want my opinion, I would go for the mini vibe. It's great to use alone or with a partner, *and* it's small, therefore discrete as well." BB winked at me, but she was so matter-of-fact. It was like we were talking about the weather, not freaking sex toys.

"All right, let's do that then." I wasn't going to argue; she was the expert after all. There was no way I wanted anything shoved up my butt, and who wanted to eat oil off of someone?

She smiled cheekily and handed it over. "Oh, and for being such a good sport, I wanted to give you this as well." She reached into a bag beside her and pulled out a paddle.

My cheeks must have been flaming red.

"Don't be ashamed. Lots of people like a little spanking in the bedroom. It's perfectly okay to enjoy being paddled."

Yeah, maybe for you. I didn't dare say that out loud, though. I leaned forward. "How did you know?" I whispered like other people were in the room who might hear my secret.

"I have a keen sense for this stuff." She

winked, and it was as effortless as her breathing. "So, what were you thinking of ordering? Or did you have questions before you decide?"

"Only one. Can I have it shipped? I would prefer not to take anything home with me tonight."

"Of course. That's not a problem." Her smile was sweet and innocent, but clearly, that wasn't the case.

Thank God. "I was thinking of ordering something similar to what you're wearing as well as the Valentine's Day package you showed at the end." I looked down at my hands, wringing them together in my lap. I couldn't believe I was doing this.

She patted me again, and somehow that calmed my nerves just a bit. "I think that's an excellent choice, especially for someone looking to explore this side of themselves for the first time. Will it be a surprise for your hubby?"

"It will definitely be a surprise or a shock." I wasn't sure which at this point. "When you mentioned Valentine's Day, it got me thinking that maybe I could plan something special for us." I shrugged, wondering what I was getting myself into but hoping that BB would encourage me.

"Ooh, that sounds nice." She started to write something down but then looked back up at me again. "Hey, there's a great hotel called The Royal Duchess not too far south of us. It's beautiful, and I happen to know the owner. I bet I could pull a few strings for you."

"Yeah? That would be great." The cogs in my head were spinning over all the possibilities that a weekend away could bring. "Thank you so much."

Chapter Three

What's With the Inquisition?

By the time we'd left Lisa's house, it was close to midnight, totally passed my bedtime. I tip-toed into the house a little inebriated, trying not to wake anyone. Quiet as a mouse, I crept into our bedroom but stumbled into the bathroom, stubbing my toe. I'd had a little too much to drink, and I wasn't much of a drinker. I set my goodies from the party onto the bathroom counter before quickly brushing my teeth and stripping off my clothes. I wasn't quite ready to have a conversation about paddles and sex toys with James, so I tucked them away in my makeup drawer before heading to bed.

I was too tired to put on pajamas, so I crawled under the covers naked. James rolled over and pulled me up against him as he always did.

He hummed in my ear. "I think I like this." His warm breath against my ear caused chills to run down my spine. "How was the party?" His voice was groggy from sleep.

"It was fun. It's been a while since we've had a girls' night, so it was nice to see everyone." I rested my hand on his stomach.

"That's good, baby. Glad you had a good time."

"I love you."

"I love you, too, good night." He kissed the back of my neck before he fell back asleep.

With the amount of alcohol I'd consumed, it didn't take long for sleep to take me under.

The sound of the kid's laughter startled me awake, I shot up in bed, looking around, completely disoriented. I ran my fingers through my hair and blew out a harsh breath. I hadn't needed an alarm in years, James always kissed me good morning to start my day. Seeing the time had me panicked, I would have just enough time to get a granola bar in Lucas before he would have to be on the bus.

My head felt a little woozy, but at least it wasn't pounding, and for that, I was thankful for, especially since I'd be rushing this morning. I threw on the first pair of leggings I could find and went to Lucas's room to wake him for school, but he wasn't there.

I walked down the stairs, and as I rounded the corner, I could see James making breakfast as the kids giggled at the television screen.

Holy crap, it's Sunday.

"Good morning, beautiful," James said as I approached. "What's wrong?" His brow furrowed as he looked down at me.

Blushing at the realization that I was going to sound like a complete moron, I looked down. "I woke up in a panic, thinking it was Monday and I was late. I nearly had an anxiety attack." I covered my face, embarrassment.

"Aw baby, come here." James knew I was a total control freak in every aspect of my life—and I owned up to it—and he must have understood that this type of thing would throw me for a loop.

I needed to destress for a little bit before I got my day on track.

James kissed my forehead and turned to make me a cup of coffee. "Here, this should help."

The feel of the warmth from the mug had me relaxing almost immediately. "God, I love you." I kissed him chastely before sitting at one of the bar stools.

After the second cup, I could feel the calm spread over me. My day would be salvaged, and I could get everything done for the day, not that I had a ton to do on a Sunday other than cleaning, laundry, and groceries, but still.

"Stacey texted and asked if she could take the kids for a bit today. Do you mind?"

James's sister was the sweetest, and I'd never tell her no. Plus, I could get my chores done super quick without the kids around, and they wouldn't be bored with her.

"Of course, that would be great."

"Okay, I'll let her know she can grab them after breakfast."

James sighed as he dropped down onto the couch

after the kids left. I sat down next to him, and he pulled me into his side.

"What shall we do today now that we have no kids?" His deep voice ran through me, and the first thought was to climb onto his lap and ride my husband, but I tamped that down.

I didn't think I'd ever initiated sex in all the years we'd been together. I needed to figure out all these new feelings, maybe I was having a quarter-life crisis or something. "I have some boring housework to do, but that's it. What were you thinking?" My mind shifted to the items I knew were in my planner's to-do list.

"Nothing specific, maybe we could go to lunch or to a movie? Just get out of the house." He rubbed his hand up and down my arm and kissed the top of my head.

"Sounds good, let me get started on my list. It shouldn't take more than a couple hours."

"Great, I have some work I need to get done in my office as well."

The tidying, scrubbing, and folding kept my mind occupied for the next couple hours—that was until James went to take a shower. All I could think about was his showering on the other side of the wall.

The water glistening down his tanned, muscular body…The way the suds would catch on in the dips of biceps, pecs, and abs—*what was wrong with me?*

I was able to get a grip and finish the housework—even getting through my own shower without dirty thoughts—before we headed to lunch. The restaurant was packed, but we were able to snag a table tucked in the corner overlooking the canal. Brio was one of my favorite Italian restaurants. Their service was impeccable, and their food was to die for. They brought our drinks and took our orders within minutes of being seated.

"So, you got in late last night. I know we talked a little bit when you got home, but I was in a sleepy fog. What was it like?" He seemed genuinely curious, but I wasn't sure how to talk about this just yet, especially not in a public place.

I looked up over my wine glass, swallowing hard. Last night was easier to answer him while in the dark and knowing he was sleepy, but now that he was looking me in the eyes, I couldn't lie to him.

Taking a sip of my wine, I bought myself

another second. "It was fun, a little out of my comfort zone, but I had a good time."

He would know something was up based on my repeated sentiments, but I took another sip from my glass and waited.

He seemed to ponder his words before continuing, "Did you buy anything?"

That wasn't a question I hadn't been anticipating, and I nearly spit out my wine. Thankfully, I was able to swallow without his realizing I'd nearly choked to death. I wasn't ready to tell him, and seeing as it was a surprise give for him, I decided it was all right to keep it a secret...so I didn't lose the shock value.

I batted my lashes. "A lady never tells."

He chuckled. "Well, considering I'm the only man you'd be using any of those toys with, shouldn't I be the only one you tell?" His smile told me he was teasing, but his eyes were dying for information.

"I won a couple things. Well, one thing, the other was given to me by the woman who ran the party."

"Oh yeah?" He was intrigued now; I couldn't help but wonder if he was thinking things were boring in the bedroom, and this would help.

However, I was terrified to ask because I was afraid of the answer.

"Yeah, I won a game." I wasn't sure how to tell him this, but I did it anyway. "They played a game about sexual *adventures*. Well, seeing as I don't really have any, I was the *winner*." I used air quotes around the word to emphasize my point. "The lady who ran the party paddled me."

His brows shot up in surprise. "Is that so?"

"I know, crazy right. I bent over and took it like a champ." I said with confidence, a little proud of myself. "She gave it to me, telling me that she could tell I liked it." The last bit slipped out, and I knew what was coming next.

His brow dipped and furrowed. "Did you?"

I took a big gulp from my glass and could've kissed the waitress when she arrived just in the nick of time with our food.

He must've forgotten all about our conversation, or at least I hoped he had. I wasn't sure how I would've told him that I'd gotten excited over being spanked with a piece of wood...hard.

Chapter Four

So That's What it Does

James hadn't mentioned the party again, and for that, I was grateful. I wasn't sure how much more of his questioning I could take before I spilled all the intimate details. I hated keeping things from him, but I really needed to sort through everything in my head before I brought anything up to him.

Jane was spending the day with her grandma, so I hoped to have time to reflect for a while after getting some things done. After ordering the groceries—I hadn't had a chance to yesterday—I made another cup of coffee and sat out on the back porch wrapped in a wool blanket. It was chilly, but I needed some fresh air.

My cell phone interrupted my thoughts with

an unknown number. I contemplated ignoring it, but when my kids weren't with me, I worried that something could be wrong. "Hello?" I waited with bated breath.

"Hey, girl. This is Betty; how are you?"

My shoulders sagged as the tension was melted from them. "Good, thanks, how about you?"

"Great! I just wanted to give you a call to let you know that I spoke with my friend over at The Royal Duchess, and you'll never believe it. He had a Valentine's Day package cancellation, and he owed me *big time*. I was able to get you the whole shebang for two-hundred bucks for the entire weekend. Can you believe that?" Her excitement was contagious.

I don't know where a woman her age got the energy, but I could only hope I was the same way. "Wow! I can't thank you enough, Betty. I owe you one." I'd looked online at the prices for that hotel, and they were in the upward of three-hundred dollars a night, and that wasn't for a fancy suite.

"You don't owe me anything, but you do have to make me a promise." She waited for my reply before continuing.

"Okay..." I wasn't sure I liked the sound of that.

"I want you to take the weekend to explore with your husband. Do some research or ask me anything you can think of. Then take everything you've bought and completely let loose. My promise to you is that you won't regret it." She sounded so sure of herself; I, on the other hand, wasn't as confident.

"I'll try my best. Ever since the party, my head's been reeling. I have so many questions I need to find answers to, but I need to dig deep to find the key to it all." I sighed, not understanding how Betty had a way of pulling the truth from me.

"I get it. I really do. You'll find a balance, and it'll all work out in the end. I think once you let go and just *feel* that everything will fall into place."

I knew she was right. I was probably over-thinking as I always did.

"Have you tried any of your goodies you won at the party?"

I swallowed hard. "Umm...no."

"Let me guess, you threw them in the back of

your underwear drawer and haven't looked at them since?"

I wasn't sure how she knew. "You're pretty close; it was my makeup drawer."

"I'll give you some more unsolicited advice. Knowing your own body is important. You need to know what makes *you* tick. Have a little fun. You may surprise yourself."

I'd never used a toy in my life, but she did say it was a good starter. "I'll try my best." I smiled at my phone. I wasn't sure where to begin, but I'd give it a go.

"That's all we can do, sweetie." She rattled off the details for the hotel for me as I wrote everything down.

I called the hotel right away and made the arrangements as Betty instructed, as well as my in-laws, to arrange for them to watch the kids and asked them to keep it a surprise. I sat there, staring at my phone after I'd hung up. I had so many mixed emotions.

I was excited about a weekend away. We hadn't done it in so long, but I was also nervous about how James would react. On the one hand, he was a *guy*. What guy wouldn't appreciate his wife in lingerie, spicing up the bedroom a little?

But on the other hand, maybe he liked things how they were, and it could turn him off. I was sure that the former was the case, but there was still a possibility I was wrong.

I tip-toed to my bedroom—which was ridiculous since I was home alone—but I felt so naughty. I took the mini vibe out of the drawer, giving it a wash, and then dropping it on the bed in front of me. I stared at it, unsure of how I felt about it. Truth be told, I wasn't even sure what to do with it.

I opened my phone and switched it over to private browsing. I wasn't very tech-savvy, so I wasn't sure if what I searched would show up on other devices. That's all I needed was for one of the kids to pick up an iPad and there's their mother's search history.

I did a quick search for the mini vibe and clicked videos. A few popped up, but they were mostly reviews from people who clearly knew what they were doing. The testimonials were good, so that was encouraging, but I needed to figure out how to use it. So, I did another search for something I'd never searched before—porn sites. I clicked the first one and searched for the mini vibe there. There were a ton of them. The thumbnails on the videos were rather graphic, but I clicked forward. I wasn't about to chicken out now.

The video started to play, and I was captivated from the beginning. A young woman laid on the bed, her head propped up on a pillow. Her legs were spread wide with the camera pointed straight between her thighs. I wasn't quite sure why, but she had her finger in her mouth. You'd think it would look stupid, but it was sexy. She reached down with one hand and picked up the vibrator that looked just like mine and switched it on. Slowly, she ran it across her nipples. She moaned softly and then moved on to the other.

I pressed paused on the video. I couldn't believe how turned on I was. James and I had slept together last night—it was Sunday after all—was I really going to do this?

I stripped down before grabbing the vibrator and getting comfortable, just like the girl in the video.

I pressed play again, and she began moving it down her body, her eyes never leaving the screen. It was like she was watching me, begging me to join her. I pushed the little switch up, and it came to life in my hand. I held it for a moment, getting a feel for it, and then mimicked the woman on the screen.

I started with my nipples, and a slight moan escaped my mouth, surprising myself as I was always quiet in the bedroom. I watched the screen as I moved it down my body, and the moment it touched my clit, I nearly combusted. The sensation was like nothing I'd ever felt before. I threw my head back, unable to focus on my phone any longer. The sound of her moans mixed with the sensation against my clit had me screaming out in pleasure as I came harder than I ever had before.

My thoughts ran wild as I laid there, panting, trying to calm my racing heart. I couldn't believe what I'd just done. I had feelings ranged from excitement to embarrassment and shame.

I had decided not to overthink it. I hopped in the shower to quickly rinse off the stench of my orgasm before going about my day. By the time the kids got home, I'd scrubbed every surface raw.

I heard the front door as James walked in. I'd almost forgotten about my romp in the bedroom earlier today. But the shame crept back in as soon as I heard the sound of his feet on the hardwoods behind me. I turned around as he strode into the kitchen and continued fixing dinner as he talked to the kids about their day.

"And how was your day beautiful?" He wrapped his arms around me from behind and kissed my neck as I kept preparing the salad for dinner. His breath on my neck gave me chills, and I had the sudden urge to take him upstairs, but I tampered down the desire.

"I kept busy, how was yours?" My mind was on an emotional roller coaster, from wanting to rip off his clothes, to being riddled with guilt. The guilt part was ridiculous, it was my body. It wasn't like I'd cheated on him.

I needed to get a grip.

"Mmm..." He breathed against my neck again. "You made my favorite, and it smells amazing."

I nodded without a word.

He chuckled against my neck. "Are you buttering me up, or did I forget a special occasion?"

"No, I just felt like making shepherd's pie and fresh bread with how chilly it was outside today."

"I'm going to wash up before dinner." He

kissed my cheek before heading upstairs. "I'll be right down."

Once the kids were down for the night, the silence crept in. Usually, I reveled in the peace and quite the evenings brought, but tonight all I wanted to do was take my husband to bed. Every move he made felt sexier, his voice seemed husky and deep, causing my insides to clench each time he spoke.

I was standing in my closet, debating on what pajamas I was going to put on— which I'd never done before—when I decided to just go for it. I chose the sexiest set I had—silk—the bottoms had a lace trim, and the tank had tiny straps. They weren't all that sexy, but they showed the most amount of skin. I went downstairs with all the confidence I could muster and detoured to the kitchen to grab two glasses and a bottle of wine.

As I walked into the living room where James was relaxing on the sofa in front of the fireplace, my confidence flew out the window. But it returned with a vengeance the second he looked up. His eyes said everything I needed to know, he wanted me, too.

I lifted the bottle and asked in the sweetest voice I manage, "Wine?"

He cocked a brow and reached for the bottle. "Allow me." He poured us both a glass as I sat down beside him. He rested his hand on my knee while he took a sip from his glass.

My lady bits tingled, and I downed mine as quickly as I could without raising any red flags. I wasn't much of a drinker, so I needed to watch it. "So..." I wasn't sure what to say, but the silence was deafening.

"So..." Clearly, he wasn't sure where to start, either. "I landed the Worthington account today."

"Wow, congratulations. I know how hard you've worked on that." I leaned over and hugged him, as I always would to show him how proud I am of him. The smell of his cologne hit me like a ton of bricks, and I couldn't help but press my lips to his.

He hesitated at first, unsure of how to react, but when I didn't pull back and instead leaned farther into the kiss, he wrapped his arm around my waist and pulled me flush against him. I opened for him, and our tongues danced together as I became more excited.

The sounds of stirring that came from Jane's baby monitor had us both frozen, waiting to see if she was going to wake. James looked into my eyes, most likely planning his next move.

I leaned across his body and took his wine glass, setting both of them on the table. Jane settled, and James hadn't moved. So I took it upon myself to take the initiative. I straddled his lap and took his face in the palms of my hands. I looked into his lust-filled eyes before devouring his mouth. I didn't hold back and took control like I'd never done before.

James's hands were all over my body like he couldn't get enough. He finally settled on my neck as he pulled me back and kissed his way down my throat. I leaned back, resting my hands on his thighs, giving him full access to my breasts. He didn't miss a beat as he pulled at the laces on the front of my tank top, exposing my breasts to him.

"Fuck," he murmured just before he took my nipple into his mouth, sucking hard.

I cried out at the onslaught of sensation. James had always been a gentle lover, but he was showing another side of himself tonight. I ground into his thickening cock beneath me as he continued to work my nipples.

"James, I need you." I panted. I couldn't wait any longer. "Now!"

He looked up at me with a devilish grin on his face. He didn't break eye contact as he reached down, pushing my pajama bottoms to the side and swiftly inserting two fingers. I threw my head back on a moan, thrusting my breasts back at James, who took full advantage.

He worked my clit with his thumb as he curled his fingers, hitting that sweet spot. I shamelessly rode his hand, quickly falling over the edge as I came. James continued sucking and nibbling on my nipples as I came down from my orgasm. When I pulled myself upright, he tried to shift me off his lap, but I stood instead and shimmied out of my shorts.

The look of complete shock on his face when I got down on my knees in front of him was priceless and spurred me on even more. My mouth watered when I pulled down his pants and he sprang free, thick and hard and oh so ready for me. I gripped his shaft and licked him from root to tip before taking him deep into my throat. His hand went to the back of my head, and he wrapped my hair in his fist, the sting excited me —which surprised me.

James guided my head, urging me to go faster and deeper as he moaned out his pleasure. But he didn't let me continue; he pulled me up. I glanced at him questioningly, but I didn't need an answer. He wanted inside of me, and I couldn't agree more.

I climbed onto his lap, positioned myself over his length, and sank down until he bottomed out inside of me. I sat there motionless for a moment while I stared into my husband's eyes. We were both seeing another side of each other. And I think we liked what we saw.

Without a word, I started to move my hips, and he gripped my face roughly before taking my mouth with a wildness he never had before. We rocked in unison as we brought ourselves to the edge and over, our moans being muffled by our passionate kisses as we both reached the top of the orgasmic mountain and jumped off hand in hand—or, in this case, dick in pussy.

James laid back on the sofa, and I collapsed onto his shoulder, completely spent.

"That was..." He kissed my forehead softly. "Amazing."

I giggled, keeping my face hidden from view,

suddenly feeling a little shy after how I'd let myself go sexually. I'd never done that before.

"Are you okay?" His concern had me taking a deep breath.

I knew we were going to have to have a conversation about this, but I was just hoping it wouldn't be right away. I sat up and looked James in the eyes. "Yes, why wouldn't it be?" I wasn't lying, everything was good.

"Don't take this the wrong way because I'm definitely not complaining, but what was that?" The smile on his face told me it was more a compliment than anything, so I took it as such.

"I don't know." I shrugged, trying to play it off like it was no big deal. "Ever since I got the invite to Lisa's party, Amy's been messing with my head."

"How so?" He eyed me suspiciously.

I couldn't believe we were going to have this discussion while he was still inside of me, but I guessed we were. "Well..." I swallowed hard. "We got to talking about our sex lives, and she kind of made fun of me for how we schedule sex. Then she found out we don't use toys, and she had a field day with that." I was embarrassed to admit that my best friend had gotten under my skin and brought us to this place, but maybe it would be the best thing that had ever happened for our marriage.

He chuckled. "Baby, are you bored with our sex life?"

I shook my head, but he could tell there was more to it as he brushed my hair behind my ear.

"You know you can talk to me, right?"

"Yeah, well, I'm not bored, but I got to wondering if you were. Then I started thinking about how we could mix things up a bit. The kids are getting a little older, so they're more consistent in their sleep schedules." I shrugged and averted my eyes for just a second. "So, we don't really need a schedule."

The smile on his face was reassuring, so I continued. "I have a confession to make." I covered my face; I couldn't believe I was going to admit this. I was sure my cheeks flamed beet red and not from the orgasm I'd just had. I took a deep breath before looking up at him. I could see the fear in his eyes, so I caressed his cheek. "So, at the party, I won two items." I dropped my head to his shoulder. "Ugh, this was so embarrassing."

"It's okay, baby; you can tell me anything."

I sat up straight and just blurted it all out,

about the paddling, the playtime earlier, everything.

He burst out laughing. "Is that it?"

What the hell? "Why are you amused by this?"

"I thought you were going to tell me you had cheated on me or something." He sighed dramatically. "Holy shit, that's such a relief."

I smacked his chest playfully. "Why the heck would you think that? Are you nuts? I felt like using that toy was like cheating. There's no way I'd ever step outside of our marriage. That alone left me riddled with guilt all day."

He chuckled again. "That's ridiculous. Masturbating is perfectly normal." He was so nonchalant about the whole thing like this wasn't the most awkward conversation ever.

"Well, I, for one, never do it." I shrugged.

He eyed me suspiciously.

"Wait, do you?" My eyes must've looked as big as saucers.

"Of course, I do. I don't know a guy who doesn't. Like I said, it's natural."

"Wow, I had no idea." I didn't know whether to feel relieved that James had secrets, too, or upset that maybe our Sunday sex wasn't enough to keep him satisfied. "I feel like I've opened up a can of worms by going to that sex party." I giggled nervously, knowing it was true—one small thing had changed so much.

"So...about that paddle." James slapped my ass playfully, and I yelped.

"Down boy, one step at a time."

"Fair enough." He kissed me softly. "I love you."

"I love you, too. I'm happy we talked."

"Me too, and I'm really glad for that sex. Damn, Riss, that was hot."

I felt the blush creep up my neck as the thoughts of what we'd just done flashed through my mind. "That was pretty tremendous."

"I think you're right, though. There's no need for a schedule anymore. This is so much more fun." His hands gently made their way down my back and landed on my ass. "And I won't lie, I can't wait for you to let me bend you over and use that paddle. Spanking your ass excites the hell out of me."

Chapter Five

Weekend Away

I'd just put Jane down for her nap when the doorbell rang. I wasn't expecting anyone, so when I opened the door to find the UPS driver, I was happily surprised. I love receiving packages. But when I looked down at the box, I was mortified. I knew that the driver had no clue what it was—the packaging had no indication of what was inside—but the fact that I knew he was holding a whole bunch of sex toys had me holding in the schoolgirl fit of laughter.

I succeeded in taking the package with only a small snicker, but it took everything in me not to burst out laughing. I managed to thank the guy, but that was all I could muster. Since Jane was sleeping, I took the package to my room and placed it on the bed. I stared at it for a minute. It seemed much bigger than I remembered. I finally gathered the courage to open it, and now I could see why it was a bigger box. There were a few more items in there than I'd ordered, so I checked the packing slip, but it seemed to be in order.

I pulled everything out one by one and set aside the additional items. There was a pair of panties, a toy cleaner, and handcuffs. My eyes went wide at the sight of the cuffs—that I was positive I hadn't ordered. I'd have to check with Betty later on that one.

I opened the corset and leatherette pants try those on to make sure they fit since I planned on surprising James with them. I noticed that the panties matched the corset, so maybe they came as a set. I opened the panties as well and burst out laughing. They were crotchless, literally had a big slit down the middle with some little ribbon ties. I couldn't breathe; I was laughing so hard. "What have I gotten myself in to?" Shaking my head, I put them on anyway, figuring, what the hell.

The last week had been amazing, and with Valentine's Day just around the corner, my nerves were completely shot. I wasn't sure if this was helping or making things worse. I was extremely excited for our weekend away. I'd made a promise to myself that I was going to let loose and just allow things to happen. I'd also decided to bring the paddle since it seemed to arouse James. So, a pair of crotchless panties was just an added bonus, right?

The get-up fit like a glove, but it was definitely missing something, walking into my closet, I zeroed in on the one pair of shoes that were a must for this outfit, my black patent leather Louboutin's. Standing in front of my full-length mirror, I was turning myself on. James was going to die when he saw me in this; I couldn't wait.

I ran my hands down my body. The lace of the corset was soft; it felt nice. I watched as I touched myself, and without thinking, let my hand roam into my pants before beginning a rhythm of slow circles around my clit. It was teasingly at first, but I became impatient, needy. I wanted to come, no, I needed to.

Watching my reflection in the mirror heightened the experience, and the sexy outfit was the icing on the cake. I leaned back against the wall as my legs became weak and pushed myself over the edge, muffling my moans of pleasure as best I could. My cheeks were flushed, and I had a slight sheen of sweat on my face—it looked good on me. After catching my breath and coming down from my orgasm, I slipped out of the outfit and cleaned up before putting my leggings and hoodie back on.

I went about wrapping the box of goodies since I was going to have James unwrap it all for Valentine's Day. I was going for shock factor at this point, and I thought I was going to surprise the hell right out of him.

I'd decided not to tell James about this weekend. He knew I had something planned but no details whatsoever. He'd tried to get it out of me, but my lips were sealed.

The weekend rolled around faster than I'd thought, and my stomach was in knots. I wasn't sure how things were going to go, but I figured we both loved each other. So no matter what, the weekend would be great.

James sat in the driver's seat. "So, where are we headed?"

I'd decided to navigate instead of drive

because I'd never been where we were headed. "South," was all I said as I buckled my seatbelt.

He smirked but didn't say a word as he took off out of the driveway toward the highway. The drive took us a little over two hours since we hit the Friday night rush hour, but we had fun singing to some oldies in the car.

I looked over at my husband as we pulled up to the valet. He really was my best friend. The anxiety I'd been feeling over the weekend melted away as I realized that there was no one else in the world I'd want to share my life with.

When the car came to a stop, I leaned over and kissed him. "I love you."

"I love you, too, baby." He smiled down at me and kissed my nose.

A tap on the window interrupted our moment, so we got out of the car, and the bellhop grabbed our belongings. The lobby was gorgeous, with rose flower arrangements everywhere to commemorate Valentine's Day.

He pulled me close to his side as we waited to check-in. "Wow, baby, you really went all out."

"I got an amazing deal through a new friend."

"May I help the next guest?" An older plump

woman said as she raised her hand slightly to signal us.

We gave her our names and credit card to get everything rolling. "*Oh*, I see you're in the Fantasy Suite in the Vanilla Wing. What a great room. You're going to love it." She smiled, and her eyes sparkled with something I was afraid to identify.

"That sounds...interesting," James muttered.

"Here are your wristbands. Please wear them for the duration of your stay. The details of the package booked are in this folder." She handed us a large envelope with quite a few papers in it. "Your key cards are in the package as well." She placed a floor plan on the counter to show us where our room was. "We hope you enjoy your stay. Please don't hesitate to contact us for anything."

"Thank you." I couldn't wait to see our room. It'd been quite a while since we'd done anything like this, so it was nice to get away.

We got off the elevator on the twelfth floor and followed the arrow that pointed to the Vanilla Wing. Each wing was named a different color: Ebony, Crimson, and Emerald, and it looked like the décor matched.

"Ah, now I get it."

Everything in our wing was cream-colored, from the carpet to the ceiling, even the paintings were different shades of the same. James opened the door to our room and motioned for me to enter first.

My jaw nearly hit the floor—it was exquisite. Everything was over the top luxurious, and I wanted to touch it all. I walked through the suite —which was huge, more like a small apartment— running my hand along the fabric and furniture. "I could get used to this."

James chuckled behind me.

We had a beautiful home, but this, this was something out of a magazine.

"I'm going to love taking advantage of this." I turned around to see James lying on the bed.

"Is it comfortable?"

"It is, but I meant that." He pointed to the ceiling.

I looked up to find the biggest mirror I'd ever seen. "Why would they have a mirror above the bed." My cheeks flushed the moment the words left my mouth. "Why would they have that in a hotel?"

The smile on his face was adorable. "So that

husbands like me can watch their sexy wives as we make love." Playful James was out for the weekend, and that was thrilling.

"Is that so?" I walked over to the bed and climbed up, straddling his lap. I flipped my hair out of my face and caught a glimpse of a large metal ring attached to the bedpost. Turning, I looked at the other posts and noticed each post had one. Sitting up, I pointed at one. "What are those?"

"Who knows?" He shrugged. "They definitely added some weird décor mixed in with how lavish this place is. For instance, look at that weirdly shaped chaise lounge over there. Like how would it be comfortable to sit on that? And it's got such a huge dip in the middle that only one person could sit there."

"You're right. I thought it was just for looks." My stomach growled, interrupting our musings.

"That's all the cue I need to feed my wife." He pulled me down to kiss him. "Do you feel like room service, or do you want to go downstairs?"

"Room service. We can relax. I'm beat and don't get much time to just put my feet up. Maybe we can rent a movie?"

"Sounds great." He patted his pockets.

"Crap, I forgot my wallet in the car. I'm going to go grab it."

"I'll come with you."

On the way back up from the car, we were standing near the elevators with another couple who looked to be about our age.

"You guys heading to the Starter tomorrow as well?" the woman asked.

"I'm sorry?" I wasn't sure what she was talking about.

She lifted her wrist. "You have the wristband, too."

"Oh, is that what it's for? We honestly haven't had a chance to look at the information we were given."

She side-eyed who I assumed to be her husband. "You should probably read it. It's a great event, I hear." She clutched his arm. "We're pretty excited. It's our first time at this one."

"Definitely," he said with a smirk.

We all stepped into the elevator, but they got off on the third floor. The woman turned and looked James up and down. "We hope to see you there."

As the doors closed, I looked up at James and burst out laughing. "What was that?"

"I have no clue, but they are one odd couple."

Chapter Six

That was Interesting

We'd spent last night lounging around. We really didn't get to do that much together; we always seemed to be so busy. We continued the laziness into today with breakfast in bed and lounging by the indoor pool well past lunch.

James came to sit at the edge of the pool. I swam up to him, stopping between his legs and resting my arms on his thighs. "I thought that maybe we should go and try out one of the restaurants downstairs. What you think?"

"That's probably a good idea. Perhaps I should get out of the water before I turn into a prune."

He chuckled but then burst out laughing when I flipped my hands over to reveal my wrinkled fingertips.

It was already five on Saturday night, and I was getting antsy. I hadn't given him his gift, nor had I worn the outfit—I was having a great time, don't get me wrong—but things just weren't going as planned, which didn't usually bode well with me.

I threw caution to the wind and grabbed the corset, opting to skip the pleather pants and headed for the bathroom to get ready.

When I was all done, I looked into the mirror and didn't even recognize myself. I had done a smoky eye, my hair in loose curls, and even put on red lipstick. I rarely wore makeup, let alone anything that dramatic, but I loved the results and couldn't wait to see my husband's reaction. I slipped into my red bottoms and took a deep breath before exiting the bathroom.

It took James a moment before he turned around, but the reaction was worth the wait. His jaw nearly hit the floor as his eyes wandered down my body before drifting back up again to meet my stare. "You look—" his voice trailed off.

I'd left him speechless, and it felt terrific. I walked over with all the confidence in the world. "You like?" I did a little twirl, and he pulled me in close.

"I love." He leaned in for a kiss, but I turned my cheek as to not smudge my lipstick.

"You ready? Because I'm starving." My stomach rumbled at that moment, breaking James out of his trance.

"I would much rather stay here and take this off of you, but I guess I could feed my wife first." He kissed my cheek again before slapping my ass.

We'd heard there was a really great French restaurant on the fourth floor, so we went in search of it.

As we turned a corner, a doorman stepped forward. "The Starter's in here."

Our confused looks must have clued him in to the fact that we weren't sure what he meant.

"You have the wristbands. The event is just starting, come on in." His friendly smile had me pause, and I looked over at James in question.

"We were on our way to dinner." James wasn't sold.

I think he just wanted to get dinner in me

and take me back upstairs, but I was kind of curious about this party since that couple was so excited about it.

"We have some great appetizers going around, drinks are flowing, and it's all included. It can be just what it's named for, your *starter* before dinner."

James sighed and looked down at me. "What do you think?"

"Sounds like fun. We can mingle for a few before dinner." I smiled at the gentleman as he opened the door for us.

Walking into the room, I had to allow my eyes time to adjust. It was too dark to see where we were going. There was club-style music playing, but at a lower decibel than any club would choose. A server approached with a tray full of hors d'oeuvres in hand. We took a plate and a few bites to eat before selecting a glass of champagne from the server, who approached from the other direction.

There were couples all around, ready to start their Valentine's Day off right as well. We walked around for a little bit before settling in at a high-top table with four stools, opting to sit close to each other. A few couples approached us, striking up conversations. I knew this hotel was luxurious, but it seemed like people had come from all over the state for this event. They all seemed nice enough, asking questions and genuinely appearing interested in the answers.

When the couple from yesterday approached, I tensed a little. James seemed to notice, so he wrapped his arm around my waist and leaned in a little closer.

They introduced themselves by name this time, Alex and Jenna. "Mind if we have a seat?" Jenna asked.

James motioned without a word and ran his hand down my spine, resting it at the small of my back where he began to trace small circles with his thumb. I rolled my eyes internally at my friendly husband, who could never tell someone no—not that I could have, either.

Surprisingly they weren't weird like I'd thought. We really hit it off and had a great time talking to them. It turned out that they live only a short distance from us.

Jenna and I went to the ladies' room together. When we came back to the table, there were more drinks there waiting. James's eyes suddenly went wide, and when I sat down, I found what he was staring at. The room was dark, but our eyes had adjusted. You could see a few couples around the room were getting frisky. I was sure that wasn't what the hotel had in mind when they thought about this event as a *starter,* but to each their own.

We had another couple of drinks and then decided it was time to dance. I couldn't remember the last time we'd been dancing, but it felt good. James's arms had pulled me in close, and his leg was between mine as we moved our bodies to the rhythm. His hands roamed my body more than he ever had in a public place. I wasn't one for PDA, but with the alcohol I'd had, I didn't mind. I was enjoying the naughty feeling that we were a little like exhibitionists. I was sure no one was watching us anyways, so I closed my eyes and enjoyed the sensation it gave me as his thigh rubbed against the apex of mine, and his hand gripped my ass firmly.

"I'm so fucking hard right now." James's husky voice mixed with his foul language had me pulling back in shock. It was hot, but it wasn't like him to curse.

I leaned in and nipped his earlobe. "Oh yeah?"

He shifted slightly, and there was no doubt that he was hard as a rock. I couldn't miss it. "There's something about the atmosphere in here that has me so turned on. I could bend you over that couch right there while everyone watched."

I swallowed against the lump that had formed in my throat. My panties dampened at the thought—although I wouldn't do it—the idea alone was enough to turn me on. I reached down and gripped James through his pants. His hiss was barely audible, but I heard it.

His leg pressed firmly against me as we rocked back and forth. "I think we should skip dinner."

"I couldn't agree more." I pulled away first and took his hand, leading him off the dance floor.

I debated on passing by Alex and Jenna without a word, but my manners got the best of me, and I stopped. "We're going to head to bed; we're exhausted." I wasn't a very good liar, and clearly, they knew I was full of it.

Jenna glanced down at my husband's crotch,

and she smirked. "Exhausted, huh? Looks like you're going to *be* exhausted later on."

James shifted on his feet but didn't bother adjusting himself. "Maybe we will see you tomorrow. Have a great night."

"You too, buddy." Alex reached out and shook James's hand and kissed my cheek.

Jenna leaned in for a hug and whispered in my ear, "Have fun tonight." She pulled back and winked.

We nearly ran back to our room. It took everything in me not to jump him in the elevator, but I deemed it inappropriate to do so with two elderly couples in front of us.

The moment the door closed behind us, I was on him, climbing him and wrapping my legs around his waist. His hands gripped the back of my thighs as he carried me to the bed. He dropped me onto the mattress, and I giggled, the laughter dying almost immediately when my husband started to undress. He didn't take his time, but I savored the view. James didn't work out much, but he took care of himself. His abs rippled as he opened his shirt to remove it; his arm muscles worked as he undid his belt, and his cock sprang free the moment his boxers allowed.

My mouth watered, and I pulled myself up onto my elbows to get a better look.

"Like what you see?" A cocky smirk graced his face, adding to the appeal.

I bit my lip and stared shamelessly at him. "Yes." The single word came out in a whisper.

"Good." He slowly approached the bed. "You have on too many clothes."

I started to take off my shoes. "Maybe we should take care of that."

"I want those back on." The glint in his eye told me everything I needed to know. This was a new James coming out to play, and I loved every second of it.

I made quick work of removing my clothes and putting the pumps back on, as he had requested. He gripped a heel in each hand, spreading my legs wide.

Unabashedly I allowed him to ogle me as I had him. "You like what you see?"

That sexy smirk returned, and I squirmed under his gaze. "Hell, yes."

I took a deep breath and decided to be more vocal than ever before. "James..." I broke him out of his daze, and he looked up at me.

"Yeah?"

"I want you to fuck me—hard."

His eyes went wide, and his cock twitched. "Turn around."

I hadn't expected that to be his response, but I did as he commanded. We'd never done it doggy style before. We always faced each other, but I was excited about something new. I rolled over and got up on all fours. James climbed onto the bed behind me and placed his open palm on the small of my back before slowly moving it up toward my shoulders as he increased the pressure, forcing my upper body into the mattress and my ass up high.

I couldn't wait any longer. "James, now."

"Shh. Let me admire the view."

This was most definitely a side he'd never seen before. I wasn't one to spread wide for all to admire, but his words and the look in his eye would've had me doing just about anything.

Both of his hands slowly worked their way back toward my bottom, and he gripped both cheeks, spreading me wide. I could feel his hot breath against my clit, and a shiver ran through me. His tongue swirled ever so gently against me before sweeping all the way up to circle my puckered hole. My body tensed, but he moved back down to my clit and slipped a finger inside me.

The moan that escaped my throat could probably be heard down the hall, but I couldn't care less. I needed him right where he was. I turned my head and locked eyes with him over my ass before reaching back and gripping his hair, keeping him right where I wanted him. "Mmm, just like that."

His eyes blazed with heat as he lapped at my juices, I collapsed back down onto the mattress, no longer able to hold myself up. James pulled back, and before I could look back to see what he was up to, he sank into me—deep. I cried out in pleasure as he stretched me wide. He didn't give me a moment to adjust; he thrust hard and fast, which was exactly what I wanted and needed at that moment.

James had always been gentle, but tonight was different. It was about something new.

His hand came down on my ass with a faint smack, I didn't flinch. I pressed back into him, urging him on without words. The next time his hand came down, it stung, but I moaned out in pleasure at the bite of his palm meeting my flesh.

"You like that, don't you?" His voice was gruff as he continued to pound into me.

"Yes." I barely managed to get the word out.

He gripped my hips hard and maintained his punishing rhythm until we both came. Hard. James and I collapsed onto the bed, and he pulled me in to be his little spoon. "I love you," he whispered into my ear.

"I love you, too."

Chapter Seven

Clueless Couple

As I stretched my body, I had aches in places I'd never felt before, and it was amazing. I thought James and I had experienced all there was in the bedroom, but man was I wrong. Last night was out of this world, and I couldn't wait to explore more with him.

James yawned and kissed my neck from behind. "Morning beautiful."

"Good morning to you, handsome." My stomach growled, and he wrapped his arms around me.

"Looks like my wife needs some breakfast. Let's order in." He rolled over and grabbed the phone off the side table but quickly put it back down. "There's no dial tone." He got up and checked the cord, but it seemed the line was just down.

"We can get dressed and head downstairs. It's fine."

He smiled down at me. "Sounds good. I'm starving and need some coffee." He kissed my forehead.

The restaurant was packed when we arrived. They informed us it'd be a half-hour wait, but that we could sit at the bar in the meantime. Coffee was at the top of our wish list anyways, so that worked out just fine.

"Hey guys, feeling a little rough today?"

I looked over to see Jenna and Alex standing behind us. I swallowed the first sip of my coffee before responding, "Yes, extremely tired. How are you guys? Did you have a good time last night?"

"We did. Are you guys waiting for a table?" Alex asked.

"Yes, they said it would be a while, but we don't mind since we have coffee. Riss here gets a little cranky without caffeine." James laughed as I smacked him playfully on the stomach.

Jenna smiled at us sweetly. "You guys are

welcome to join us. Our buzzer just went off, and we'd asked for a booth, so we have room."

James looked at me in question.

"Sure, that would be great. Thank you." I hopped off the stool, making sure to grab my coffee.

We sat down in the booth, the guys opposite us girls. The waiter took our order almost immediately, and although I wanted to order the whole menu, I refrained.

Jenna turned to me with a smile. "So, what did you think of last night? I assume it was your first event?"

"Yes, is that something the hotel does every year? Everyone seemed so friendly. It was definitely a great start to our Valentine's."

She took a sip of her coffee before explaining. "Starter is a company that's been around for years. They host events like that on the regular. This one happened to be on Valentine's Day weekend, but it doesn't have to be. It's just a way to meet like-minded couples in your area."

"Oh, that's nice. I hadn't heard of it before. An acquaintance of mine booked this weekend for us. I had no idea what was included, but we're definitely glad we went."

Alex cleared his throat. "Would you guys be interested in more parties like *that*? We have a great group of friends that get together regularly."

I looked at James, who had a confused look on his face that most likely mirrored mine.

"What do you mean like *that*?" James asked the question that I had on the tip of my tongue.

"Swingers parties," Alex said matter-of-factly.

We sat there in silence as his words sunk in, and then I burst out laughing. "Wow, it all makes sense now." I shook my head. "Well, aren't we the clueless couple?"

James mimicked my laughter. His face was beet red. "We really are."

"Wait, you had *no* idea? Like, *none*?" Jenna looked like she was on the verge of laughter, as well.

"Not a clue. I mean, it all makes complete sense now, but at the moment, I didn't think anything of it." I sipped my coffee, trying to hide my complete and utter embarrassment. How could we be so oblivious?

"Holy shit, everything is all making so much more sense now." James shook his head. "You guys must think we're complete morons."

Jenna placed her hand on my arm. "Not at all. If you didn't book the weekend, that's totally logical."

Alex piped in. "How do you feel about things now that you know what it really was?"

I swallowed hard, unsure of how to answer that question. I looked between James and Alex, realizing that this couple at the table most likely wanted to sleep with us.

James saved me. "I'm not sure how to even answer that. We've never discussed anything of the sort. That's a lot to take in."

"Fair enough. It's definitely not a lifestyle for everyone, but it's also not something that you do on a whim. It took a lot of talking and time before we took the plunge. We have friends who have been in the lifestyle for years, some like us, are newer, and others, who are just exploring the possibility and aren't quite ready to take the plunge yet." Alex smiled at me before looking at James. "We would love it if you guys would join us next weekend. There's absolutely no pressure. We hang out, have drinks, food, play games, just like every other party."

I wasn't sure what to say, so I blurted out the

first thing that came to mind. "We will have to discuss it and see if we can get a sitter. We don't get out much, but not sure the in-laws can handle the kids two weekends in a row." I thought that gave us a good out if we needed it.

Jenna and Alex gave us a little bit of a rundown on things, but we basically kept things a little less personal for the rest of the conversation. We exchanged numbers and enjoyed the rest of our breakfast. It wasn't awkward like I thought it would be. They were genuinely nice people, and I loved spending time with them.

We went our separate ways after breakfast, promising to keep in touch. Check out time was nearly here, and we had to pack up our room and head home.

I think we both took the time we had to let everything marinate. It had been quiet until we got about twenty minutes into the drive and James broke the silence. "I take it your mind is racing just as much as mine is?"

I giggled nervously. "Just a little."

"It's a lot to take in." He reached over and squeezed my leg. "I can't believe we went to a swingers party and had absolutely no idea." We both laughed at the absurdity of it all, it was really surreal.

"So, what do we think about this whole party thing?" He rubbed small circles on my thigh.

I wasn't sure how to respond. I hadn't really had a chance to fully explore how I felt about it. On the one hand, I was excited about going and seeing what would happen. But on the other hand, the thought of someone else touching my husband had me wanting to scream and throw up all at the same time. I took a deep breath and decided to go with the truth.

He blew out a sigh of relief. "Oh, thank God, I feel the same way."

"It's honestly so much to take it, I feel like my head's about to explode."

He rubbed up and down my leg, knowing I would be over-analyzing everything, but I knew he felt the same way.

"I think I need to talk to Jenna a little more to make sure that there aren't any expectations that I'm not comfortable with. I also am not interested in seeing a bunch of people messing around, either. I think that could get awkward really quickly."

"Yeah, I'm not looking for a live porn show."

He smiled and side-eyed me. "Although..." He let the word trail off, and I smacked him with the back of my hand.

The conversation was a little uncomfortable, so I was grateful for him making light of the situation. "I bet you aren't." I chuckled.

Chapter Eight

Why Not?

We kissed the kid's goodnight as we walked out the door. I couldn't believe we were going to a swinger's party, but Jenna assured me there was no pressure at all, and there wouldn't be writhing bodies all over the place.

We'd kept in constant contact over the last week, and she had held my hand through every question and all my second-guessing. She assured me that she was the exact same way, except that it had taken them over a year to take the plunge.

"Are you okay?" James looked down at me as we pulled into the driveway of Jenna and Alex's house.

I smiled. "Yeah, why?"

"You've been gripping my hand like a vice the whole drive; it feels like you may have broken a few bones."

"Shut up, I have not." I stretched my hand; it was a little cramped, so he was most likely telling the truth. "Sorry, I'm just a little nervous."

"We can turn around; I don't want either one of us to feel pressured into this."

"I don't feel any pressure. It's just the unknown. I know that once I'm inside and I see it's not a sex dungeon—like I'd always expected when I thought of swingers—that everything will be fine."

He held my face in his hands and kissed my forehead. "I love you. If, for any reason, you feel like you want to leave, just give me the signal, and we're out of there."

We'd discussed an exit strategy just in case. I was a planner, so that was important. "No touching, right?"

"None. One hundred percent off the table."

I took a deep breath. "I'm ready."

As we approached the house, the front door swung open.

Jenna appeared and threw her arms open as she ran toward me. "You came!" She pulled me in for a hug, and I relaxed just a tiny amount. She pulled back, keeping me at arms-length. "Don't be nervous." She kissed my cheek. "Let's get you a drink."

James went to pull his hand from mine, thinking I was okay. I gripped it tightly, not letting him go. I wasn't quite ready. Jenna linked arms with me on my other side and pulled us into the house. It was stunningly decorated, lots of whites and greys with subtle pops of color throughout. My kids would have this place destroyed in no time.

"What's your poison?" She asked as she rounded the corner bar.

"Wine, please, I'm not picky."

She poured me a generous glass, and for that, I was grateful. She made James a drink as well and then came around to link arms with me again. "Let me introduce you to some people." She smiled at me, and I nodded.

By the time the introductions were done, we'd been there for nearly an hour. Everyone was really nice and talked to us for quite some time before we were able to move on to the next couple.

James stuck close by my side, but I was no longer breaking his fingers.

Judy—I think that was her name—suggested we play a game she'd brought called *Taboo*. The title had me a little anxious, but it was nothing like the name insinuated. It was a lot of fun.

I had noticed a few couples split off, but no one batted an eye. We continued on with the party, drinking and having a great time. James stopped after drink number two so that he could drive, and I could have a few more.

Jenna stuck to her word and stayed close by, she made me feel like I was an old friend. Alex did the same with James, although I think once we walked in the door, he was fine—cool as a cucumber. He was always easy-going, so that didn't surprise me.

We'd been at the party for a couple hours, and I was having a great time. It was easy to forget what type of party this really was, except for the biggest tell, which was how...friendly everyone was with each other.

I leaned over to whisper in Jenna's ear. "So, I have to ask, have you guys *all* slept together?"

She threw her head back and burst out laughing. I was mortified but realized that although she was amused, she wasn't laughing *at* me.

When she finally caught her breath, she turned to me and answered, "No, not all of us. Some have." She leaned in closer so that only I could hear and explained which couples were newer and just exploring like us, some had been coming for months but haven't taken the plunge yet, and then others had been in the lifestyle for a long time.

It was interesting to watch the body language of everyone and compare it to what stage they were at in their journey. It looked like Cindy and Derrick were leaning more toward taking the plunge from the way they were cozying up to Lori and Craig. To my surprise, I had no judgment in my heart about it. At that moment, I knew that no matter what decision James and I made as a couple, I was glad for this experience. It opened my mind up to something I had never even considered. Had someone mentioned it to me before, I would've done nothing but judge them. All of these people here tonight were great, honestly nicer than most I knew. Their sexual preference was no one's business but their own—

well unless you were sleeping with another couple, of course.

James had been hanging out with a few other guys while I sat with their significant others. He glanced my way often, making sure I was all right. He really was the best husband.

Chapter Nine

Expect the Unexpected

The party seemed to be winding down, but then it dawned on me that no one had left—well, not that I had noticed anyway. So, they were probably off having *fun* somewhere else.

I was starting to get a little tired, so I stood to stretch my legs for a bit and then headed for the bathroom, hoping that a splash of water to the face would help wake me up. The hallway was dark, and I wasn't quite sure where I was going. I got to the door to what I believed to be the bathroom. As I turned the doorknob, I heard rushed footsteps behind me. Before I could turn around to see who was coming, strong arms wrapped around me and pulled me in through the door. A scream caught in my throat as I was whirled around. When I saw it was my husband, I smacked his shoulder, but before I could yell at him for scaring me half to death, his lips found mine. I heard the faint click of the door before his hands gripped my ass and lifted me, pressing me into the wall.

My heart rate picked up as I wrapped my legs around him. He kneaded my ass and kissed his way down my neck.

"Wait." I pushed away slightly and shushed him. "I hear something."

We stood there, silent in the dark, and then I heard it again. A moan came from the other side of the wall and a few grunts, followed by more moaning. I giggled like a schoolgirl at the thought of someone else having sex in the next room, but my amusement turned into something else when James rocked against me. I looked down at him, his eyes were heavy-lidded, and his devious smile told me he was ready to bend me over the sink in this bathroom. I took his mouth and rubbed myself against his hard length, trying to get some relief. I moaned against his lips as I continued to work myself up.

"I need you." His voice was husky with desire.

I looked around, not sure I was comfortable with this.

He put me at ease as he lifted my chin, so I looked him in the eyes. "Not here."

"Oh, thank God." I blew out a sigh of relief.

"We can go out, make our rounds, and then say the sitter called or something."

"Sounds good to me." I was so turned on I would've walked out without saying a word at this point.

By the looks we were given as we said our goodbyes, everyone knew we were completely full of it.

We climbed into the car, and James pulled out and sped down the street quicker than he usually would. "Where to?"

I looked around, thinking about what to do next. We were about twenty minutes from home.

"Head home." I smirked at him and laughed when he furrowed his brow.

Clearly, he wasn't willing to wait, but what he didn't know was that I wasn't going to make him. I licked my lips and turned toward him, leaning over, exaggerating every movement for his benefit. I kept eye contact as long as I could and watched his frown turn into a grin, the moment he realized what I was going to do.

I slowly unzipped his pants and pulled his hard length free before licking him from root to tip. He adjusted himself in his seat, which gave me a little more room to work.

I took him in as deep as I could and then slowly worked myself back up. I got into a rhythm, speeding up slightly when the sound of a hiss coming from his lips spurred me on. He started to caress my head, gently at first, but as I picked up my pace, his movements became rougher. He then gripped my hair, hard. His actions guided mine at the pace he desired until he came with a loud grunt down the back of my throat.

I did his pants back up and started to adjust my dress in my seat, but he stopped me when I went to pull it down.

"My turn." The devilish gleam in his eye had my legs falling open without a thought, and his hand inched my dress all the way back up my thighs, exposing my red lace.

"Take them off." His deep voice ran through me, and I complied without a second thought, pulling my panties down my legs and tossing them onto the floorboard.

His hand gripped my inner thigh as he pulled it toward him, and as we slowed to a stop at the light, he leaned over, spread my lips open, and sucked hard on my clit. My head fell back against the headrest as he swirled his tongue around my sensitive bundle of nerves.

The sound of a horn behind us broke the moment, but he didn't stop there. His hand took over where his tongue had left off. I was so far gone I would've let him take me in the middle of the street at this point. His fingers continued to work me; I was so close to the edge, but he kept me teetering there.

"I need to come, James." I gripped his wrist, trying desperately to get him where I needed him.

"Not yet, baby. We're almost home, and I want you coming on my dick." His dirty words had me clenching around his fingers.

"But my parents..." I couldn't let them see me like this.

"They'll be sleeping in the guestroom. Don't worry." He assured me as he circled around my clit, narrowly—and most likely decisively—missing the spot I needed him most.

A few minutes later, we were pulling into the driveway. James leaned over and kissed me, then slowly removed his hand from between my legs with a smirk I could feel on his lips.

"Bastard."

He chuckled as he got out of the car. I took a moment to calm myself. I was wound so tightly I thought I might explode. I even contemplated making myself come before I got out. It wouldn't take much, but I decided against it.

James took my hand as we walked into the house. It was quiet and dark. I kicked off my heels, so I didn't make any noise. We quickly tiptoed through the house. The moment we entered the bedroom, James closed the door, pinned me against it, and consumed my mouth. My body needed him. I couldn't get close enough. He took my cues and lifted me to carry me to the bed, where he sat me down on the edge and spread me wide. His eyes blazed with desire as he undressed, not taking his eyes off the apex of my thighs.

I felt his thickness as he rubbed himself

against me. "Please, James." I was done waiting, and apparently, he was too.

James pushed forward to the hilt, lifting my legs to grip my ankles for leverage before he began his pounding rhythm. I couldn't catch my breath between thrusts. I never in my life thought I would like sex this way, but it was quickly becoming all I ever wanted. Hard and fast.

I could tell he was holding back, so I did something I rarely did, I told him what I needed. "Harder."

His eyes lit up as the word left my mouth, and he didn't disappoint. He picked up his pace and slammed into me, over and over. I screamed out as I came.

James collapsed on top of me as he came with a groan. "Holy…"

"Tell me about it." I was spent and utterly satisfied.

Chapter Ten

Spill it

A faint knock on the door pulled me out of my sleep, I rolled over to see my mom in the doorway.

"We're going to take the kids to breakfast and then to the park," she whispered with a smile.

"Thank you." I curled back up, not ready to get up quite yet, but James leaned over and kissed my cheek.

"I have something for you." He reached behind him and into the nightstand and pulled out a small black box. "Happy belated Valentine's Day. Our weekend got away from us, and I had completely forgotten to give this to you."

I took the box from him and began to open it slowly, all the while panicking inside about the gift I had never given him. I didn't *have* to give him anything. I was sure he thought the weekend away was his actual gift, but I was apprehensive about how he'd react to the box of toys. I opened the lid and gasped, it was a gorgeous diamond tennis bracelet that I'd been eyeing for months.

I looked up at my husband. "Thank you, it's beautiful."

"Just like you." He kissed my forehead. "That was cheesy, wasn't it?"

"A little, but I like cheesy." I took a deep breath, deciding I should give him his gift, too. "I'll be right back."

I took my time getting it, not sure how he was going to react. I slowly walked back to the bed with the big box in my arms. "I didn't get a chance to give you yours, either."

James's face was all smiles; he loved surprises. He tore at the wrapping paper like a kid on Christmas morning. "Naughty Weekend Away?" The confusion was written all over his face. "Didn't we already have that?"

"Before you open it, keep in mind this was supposed to be *for* our weekend away." I was self-conscious and unsure of myself. When I bought it, I was confident that it would be something we could explore together, but now I was wondering if I was going to insult him.

He lifted the lid slowly, and his expression told me everything I needed to know. He was in shock.

I pushed the lid closed. "We don't have to use them. It was stupid. I bought it as an impulse at the party. Betty convinced me it was something we should explore together and—"

"Riss," James cut me off. "It's not stupid, I'm just...surprised is all. We've never used toys before, and this is a *lot* of toys." His eyes were wide.

He opened the box again but didn't say anything, just looked around, checking out each item. Then suddenly, he pulled out an object shaped like the letter *u*. "This one."

I had no clue what it was or what he meant. "Huh?"

He put the box aside and walked to the bathroom, I heard the water running and then out he came, stalking toward me with a determined look on his face. He crawled onto the bed and hovered above me. "I want to try this one first."

I swallowed hard, not sure what the toy did, but I hoped he had an idea.

I'd been avoiding Amy since she got back from vacation. I didn't have a clue what to tell her and knew I couldn't keep anything from her. She was bringing over Mary, so I was a nervous wreck. I'd cleaned my house from top to bottom, and I couldn't sit still. When she walked in the door, I felt like I was going to vomit.

"Where the hell have you been?" The humor in her tone calmed me a little, but not completely.

Mary took off to the playroom, knowing she'd find Jane there.

"I've been here. What have you been up to?" My voice shook a little as I made tea with my back toward the door.

"Not much, really. We did our annual cruise, and that's about it. You guys should totally come next year." She sat down at the counter, and I set her tea in front of her. She smiled before taking a sip. "Thank you. I totally forgot. How was your weekend? You haven't said a word."

I'm sure my face was bright red at the mention of the weekend.

"Oooh, that good, huh? Your face is turning fifty shades of red right now. You need to spill."

I sighed. I knew it wouldn't take much, and I'd be spilling the beans. Amy wasn't the judgy type, but I was still nervous to tell her everything. I started off slow, just explaining my plans and then eased into how things changed quickly. Her facial expression stayed almost neutral; her eyes were the only thing that gave away her shock. I'd told her almost everything, but I left out the swinger party.

I took a deep breath and waited for her to respond, but she didn't say anything. "Can you please say something?" I couldn't take the silence.

A Cheshire size smile slowly spread across her face. "You dirty whore." We both burst out laughing at the same time. "Wow! I'm shocked, Little Miss Sunday Sex..."

I slapped her shoulder. "Shut it."

"I am truly speechless. You went from bland to spicy in less than a few weeks. Good for you." She took a sip of her tea. "So...the sex is good?"

The blush returned at her question, but I couldn't wait to tell her. "Oh. My. God. Best *ever*. I had no idea that it could be that good." I dropped my head into my hands, completely embarrassed. I'd never been one to talk about this type of personal stuff, but she was my best friend, who else was I to talk to about it?

"Eeek. Girl, I'm so happy for you."

I looked up at her and took another deep breath, I needed to tell her about the party.

"What?" The concern was written all over her face.

"There's more."

"More? *Spill.*"

And so, I did. I told her the rest, and this time, her face didn't remain neutral. The shock was plain as day. "Now, that was *not* what I had expected you to say."

She looked up at the ceiling as if contemplating what to say, and then she smiled. "Do you think Steven would agree to go to one of these parties?"

I'd never snorted so hard. "If James agreed, I can assure you that Steven would be on board."

We spent the rest of the afternoon chatting. Every once in a while, she'd randomly change the subject back to swingers and ask another question. It was kind of weird since she was the one schooling me just a few weeks ago.

By the time Amy left, I was positive that she was going straight home to ask Steven about the whole swinger thing. I was sure that she was in the same boat as I was, intrigued and unsure of how she felt about it but fascinated enough to want to check it out. Jenna had said we were welcome to bring anyone as long as we were confident that they'd be a good fit.

Chapter Eleven

Ten Cabins and a Hot Tub

The last few weeks had been amazing. I had no idea how much sex influenced our relationship. James and I had a great marriage before, but I noticed that with more openness in the bedroom came more communication. I felt a closeness to James that I hadn't felt before.

We'd kept in touch with Jenna and Alex, even going to dinner a couple times. Last week, Amy and Steven had joined us, and we all had a great time. They invited us for their annual long weekend away, and we couldn't be more excited. They'd rented out a location that had ten cabins as well as a central clubhouse.

I'd been packed for days and was now pacing

impatiently, waiting for James to get home so we could leave. He was getting off early, but it was a five-hour drive, and I wanted to get going.

"You seem excited." My mom interrupted my pacing.

"I am. This weekend should be a lot of fun." I would never dare tell my mom that technically it was a swinger's retreat because she'd most likely have a heart attack or something.

"It's nice to see you two getting out more often and spending time together." Her smile was genuine. "You were starting to worry me that you were an old married couple way too soon." She chuckled, but I could hear the truth in her tone. She'd always told me that we needed to get out more and enjoy each other's company, I always thought that spending time with the kids was enough, but I now realized just how wrong I was I needed time alone with James as well.

"Okay, I'll say it. *You were right.*" I kissed her cheek and squealed the second I heard James's car pull into the driveway.

"You kids have fun."

James came in so that he could change and say goodbye to the kids. He also helped me with the bags.

We pulled out of the driveway and were on our way within minutes of his coming home. I turned on a pop station and bopped to the music in the passenger seat.

"You're in a good mood," James remarked.

"I am. Aren't you excited about this weekend? The pictures of this place looked amazing. We haven't done anything like this...well ever."

He rested his hand on my bouncing knee. "It did look pretty great, and since they've been there before, I assume it's as cool as they made it sound."

"Too bad Amy and Steven had to bail. I hope Mary feels better soon."

Amy had called me yesterday, the disappointment in her tone was upsetting, but family first. Her little one's fever was spiking, so she wanted to stay home to be close by, which as a mom, I understood.

"Yeah, having them there would've been a bonus for sure."

The drive up didn't seem to take long, and when we pulled up, it was so much prettier than I'd expected. The lake view was breathtaking, and I couldn't wait to watch the sunset.

Jenna and Alex came out to greet us and

showed us to our cabin so that we could get situated.

Jenna closed the door behind us. "Sorry to hear that Amy and Steven had to cancel. We'll have fun either way, but it would've been nice to have them."

"Yeah, it sucks. They were really looking forward to coming, but Mary's fever wasn't letting up."

"Yeah, I get it. Well, get settled and then come meet us in the clubhouse. We're still waiting on three more couples, but they should be here any minute."

Smiling, I set down my bag on the small sofa. "Great, we will be there in a few."

They left us to it, and we checked out the bathroom before putting our bags in the bedroom.

"This place is so adorable. I love it." The cottage had a small bedroom with a queen-sized bed, a nice-sized bathroom with a soaker tub, and a makeshift living room with a loveseat, mini-fridge, and microwave.

"I take it we cook in the clubhouse since there's no kitchen?" James noted.

"Yeah, Jenna mentioned that. She wouldn't

accept any money from me for anything, so I'm hoping I can slip her a few bucks at some point without her noticing."

James laughed and reached his hand out. "You ready?"

I nodded and took his hand.

We walked into the clubhouse and were greeted by some familiar faces. This place looked newly renovated and had all the amenities you'd ever need. I had a feeling we'd be spending most of our time in here. It had high vaulted wood ceilings, floor-to-ceiling windows, and three sofas surrounding a fireplace with a flat-screen above it. The kitchen was gorgeous with a massive island surrounded by stools, and right in front of the one wall of windows was the dining room with the longest table I'd ever seen.

James went over to hang out with the guys, and I took off toward the kitchen where the girls sat at the island.

"Clarissa," they all said in unison and lifted their drinks as I walked up.

Jenna handed me my own, and we all clinked glasses. "Yay, we're all here. Time to get our drink on."

I took a sip of the best wine I'd ever tasted. "Thank you."

Cindy started up the gas stove and began taking ingredients out of the refrigerator.

I felt rude that we were all standing around while she did the cooking. "Do you need any help?"

Jenna came over and chuckled as she threw her arm over my shoulder. "Don't bother. She won't let anyone get involved."

I looked over at Cindy with wide eyes, wondering why she would voluntarily cook for so many people. She nodded and shrugged. "I love to cook, but I am a lone wolf in the kitchen."

"Fair enough." I lifted my glass to her and took another swig. "I'll be over here, enjoying this amazing wine."

We had a great time that night, drinking, eating, and just hanging out like we were all old friends—well, most of them were—but it felt like we'd been a part of the group forever. We'd made a fire and watched the sunset over the lake. It was even more stunning than I'd thought it would be.

"So, what's the plan for tomorrow?" I assumed, based on how organized Jenna was, that she had an itinerary of sorts.

She didn't disappoint. She rambled off a whole list of activities, from canoeing to hiking, and then for the evening, we would be winding down with some hot tubbing and, of course, drinking and lots of food throughout the day.

I sighed dramatically. "I'm exhausted just thinking about that."

"You'll love it, I promise."

I really wasn't the outdoorsy type, but being out here was quite literally a breath of fresh air.

"We should come up here in the summer. We could add swimming and boating to the list."

Honestly, I was freezing my ass off right now, but James was doing his best to keep me warm under our blanket. The fire was helping for sure, but it was March, and although we didn't get much of a winter, it was cold.

Jenna's eyes lit up. "Great idea, I'll start planning."

I had no doubt that she was planning everything in her head right now and was itching for a notebook and day planner to figure out the details.

Chapter Twelve

My Legs are Numb

The clock read nine when I opened my eyes, I was shocked, the fresh air must have done me some good because I slept like a rock. I stretched my arms above my head as James walked out of the bathroom.

"Do we really have to go hiking?" I whined.

He crawled up the bed with a smirk on his face. "Yes, maybe you'll like it. You never know."

"Oh, I'm one-hundred percent positive that I will *not* enjoy hiking." I rolled my eyes but stretched up to kiss him.

He pulled back before I could reach him. "Well, you can suck it up, princess, because we're going to make the most of this weekend." He leaned down and kissed me before sitting back up and smacking me on the butt. "Let's go, woman. It's time to get some coffee in you. Make sure you put some comfy clothes on and dress warmly. It's a little chilly out this morning, but once you get moving, you'll heat right up."

I threw the pillow over my face and sighed. "Can't I just stay in bed?"

"Nope, let's go."

Grumbling like a teenager, I got up and put on my leggings and flannel. Stepping out into the cold, I was surprised how nippy it was out. I just hoped the sun would bring a little warmth.

"She made it," Jenna shouted from the other side of the room.

"Unfortunately." I smacked James on the shoulder. "This one wouldn't let me stay in bed."

"Good." She walked over and handed me a cup of coffee. "There's cream and sugar on the counter over there."

"You're a Godsend." There was no way I'd survive this hiking shit without caffeine, and the blueberry muffins that sat beside the creamer looked to die for.

They didn't give me much time to savor my coffee before they were pushing me out the door. I felt like a petulant child, so I sucked it up and put a smile on my face. I was going whether I liked it or not, so I figured I might as well make the most of it.

By the time we were heading back to the clubhouse, I was spent and seconds away from begging James for a piggyback, but I wouldn't give him the satisfaction. He was waiting for me to give up, but I was too stubborn. I kept up, although my legs were now numb. As soon as I was in the clubhouse, I collapsed onto the sofa.

Cindy went straight for the kitchen and started washing her hands, gearing up to start a late lunch for everyone. I prayed it was something quick because I was starving.

Jenna collapsed beside me, resting her head on my thigh. "Girl, doesn't your body feel good after that?"

I wanted to tell her that she was insane but refrained. "Umm, I wouldn't use the word *good*. I can't really feel my legs."

She rolled over onto her elbows and looked up at me. "How could you have that banging body without working out on a daily basis?"

I just shrugged. I didn't have a *banging* body, but I was just blessed with a nice figure that I didn't have to work for. "I eat right, I guess; I like healthy foods."

"Lucky bitch." She laughed and rolled back over again.

I could barely keep my eyes open, but when Cindy said the sandwiches were ready, I nearly pushed Jenna onto the floor, I got up so fast. I limped over to the counter to make my lunch plate.

Alex came up behind me. "I think a massage is in order tonight."

I whipped my head around, surprised he was being so forward, but James was standing right there with a big smile on his face.

"I couldn't agree more." James's smile was brilliant and full of mischief, and suddenly, I couldn't wait for tonight.

"Anyone up for a game after this? We could probably all use some downtime." Tiffany looked at me with the last words, knowing I was the lightweight here.

I was grateful that she didn't bring up the canoeing that we were supposed to do because I could handle my legs and arms both being jelly. I guess I thought too soon because just then, Craig moaned about canoeing. Thank God James piped in and suggested the guys go out canoeing and the girls stay back. I was perfectly happy with that solution.

I walked over and kissed him. "Thank you."

"Of course, but you owe me for that one." He winked before kissing me again.

We spent the afternoon talking, drinking wine, and watching chick flicks instead of playing games. I had a great time, but I really wished my bestie was here for this. She would've loved it, and I felt terrible that I was enjoying myself without her, while she was stuck at home with her sick baby girl. I'd checked in with her, but she ordered me to have fun and assured me Mary was fine. In fact, she was almost back to her crazy self.

Cindy broke me out of my thoughts. "I thought that maybe we should have a bunch of appetizers for dinner to keep it simple and allow us to snack around the hot tub. What do you guys think?"

We all agreed, although, to me, it sounded like more work for Cindy. She definitely knew her way around the kitchen. So, we watched as she cooked, wrapped, sprinkled and baked some fantastic looking hors d'oeuvres and left them to keep warm while we all grabbed our suits. I felt like the librarian compared to most of the other women. I was wearing a two-piece, but it was nothing fancy. These women left nothing to the imagination—they might as well have been nude.

We slipped into the hot tub—if you could call it that—it was more like a small pool. Although it was huge, I wasn't sure how we'd all fit in there once the guys tried to get in, too, but we didn't have to wait long to find out.

They must've seen us get in and came back right away. They didn't even go to get their suits. They all jumped into the water in their boxers or underwear. A few women ended up on their husband's laps—me included—but I didn't mind at all.

"What's this?" Craig snapped his wife's strap.

"Yeah, why's everyone covering up the goods?" Mason agreed.

"It was just us girls, but now that you're here —" Cindy didn't finish her sentence. Instead, she undid her straps and lifted her swim top in the air seductively before dropping it to the ground. "Better?"

Craig pulled her nipple into his mouth and spoke around it. "Absolutely."

A few others followed suit, but some kept them on. I wasn't sure what to do. I was comfortable enough to take off my top, but I wasn't sure how James would feel, so I decided to keep it on.

The noise from the jets was loud, not that it mattered since the conversation had quieted as the couples around us started to get frisky under the water. Legs were rubbing up against mine, elbows against elbows. I had been sitting on James's lap facing outward, thinking we were all going to be chatting and drinking our wine, but after a few seconds of watching everyone else getting intimate, I realized that wasn't the case. James's hand began to run up my inner thigh, the other up my stomach to cup my breast. I sank back into him, relaxing at his touch.

In our vanilla world, we'd never done anything like this before, the excitement of having others around heightened the sensations and increased my arousal.

I looked up and caught Alex's stare as he kissed his way down Jenna's neck. His eyes were heavy-lidded, but he kept his gaze on me as James breached the edge of my bathing suit and began circling my clit. My head fell back against James's shoulder, and my mouth dropped open on a silent *oh* as I tried to keep my pleasure quiet. The corner of Alex's mouth curled up as he continued his ministrations.

The realization that someone was watching me made me feel naughty and turned the intensity up a few levels.

I was trying my best to keep quiet, but it was getting harder and harder. I turned in James's lap and straddled him, taking his mouth in hopes it would muffle my moans. I could hear the others around me, but I wasn't quite ready for them to hear me.

After coming down from my orgasm, I attempted to take care of James, but he stopped me. He leaned down and whispered in my ear. "Later." He kissed my neck, and just like that, I was ready for bed.

Chapter Thirteen

All I Need

Last night was amazing. The excitement of the hot tub, followed by the amazing sex when we got back to our cabin, I couldn't seem to get enough of my husband, and it was a great feeling.

But it was now back to reality. Saying goodbye to this weekend was hard. We'd had such a great time and made so many lasting memories with our new friends. Jenna and Alex had quickly become two of our closest friends, and I couldn't imagine them not being a part of our lives at this point. The only things missing were Amy and Steven, but I realized that I wouldn't have been as comfortable with exploring as much with them right there. They'd been in our lives for so long that it might've felt awkward, not on their side but on ours.

The drive home was long, and although I was excited to see the kids, a sense of melancholy loomed over us. My hand was cradled in James's the whole way home, as we talked about inconsequential things and listened to music. But it all felt gloomy, even the weather was on board with its miserable clouds and incessant rain.

"My mom mentioned that the kids have been cooped up in the house all weekend. What do you think about taking them to an indoor playground when we get home? We get to relax with coffee, and they can have a little fun?" I really just didn't want to sit home and do nothing and thought this was a good alternative.

"I think that's a great idea." He squeezed my hand but didn't say anything else.

The kids were ecstatic to see us and even more excited to go to the playground. They always had so much fun there. And I had to give myself a pat on the back. By the time we had gotten home from all that jumping and running, the kids were beyond exhausted and passed out.

I'd done the laundry and tidied up a bit before we went to bed. We were so exhausted ourselves from the weekend and playing with the kids that we'd called it a night early.

I'd received a text from Amy early this morning, and she'd assured me that Mary was good to go. She wanted to come over. I couldn't wait to tell her about the weekend and rub it in that they'd missed out.

When she walked in, Mary ran up to me for a hug, which was rare. She usually ran straight for Jane, so I gladly took the split second she gave me before she squirmed out of my arms to head off to play.

"Well, that was short-lived," Amy said as she sat down at the kitchen table. "So, how was the weekend?"

I knew what she wanted to know; she hadn't been to a party, so she was expecting juicy gossip. I told her every detail, feeling my cheeks flame red hot over the jacuzzi incident. Just thinking about it had me excited all over again.

"I'm so sorry I missed it; do you think Jenna will do one in the summer like you suggested?"

"Unquestionably, she's already planning it."

"We're definitely in, it sounds like so much fun, and I can't wait to meet all the other couples." She took a sip of her coffee. "So, have you and James made any decisions about whether you actually want to take it to the next level?"

I shook my head. "No, we really haven't talked much about it. We seem to be having a good time with how things are, you know? I haven't brought it up, and neither has he. But if I had to make a decision right now, I would say no. I'm not sure I would be okay with another woman touching my husband."

"And what about another man touching you?" Amy grinned over her mug at me.

"As much as the thought is exciting, something new and different, I don't think I could do it. From my understanding, most people don't just jump into the lifestyle. It can take *years* for a couple to take the plunge, so who knows where things will go."

"Want to hear my thoughts?" She cocked a brow, daring me to tell her no.

I lifted my mug, urging her to continue.

"I think neither of you is ready for the next step, and to be quite honest, I don't think you'll ever be. But I think the parties are something you guys should continue with. It's exciting and seems to do *something* for you guys. You're glowing and look so much happier than you were before, not that you weren't happy. I think you were just content, and now you're beaming, and things are great."

"Maybe." I shrugged.

James and I really did need to have a conversation about it, but there was no need to rush it. I didn't elaborate on that, and Amy didn't push. This was not something I needed to decide today, and it wasn't something I could do without my husband, either.

I tried to turn the tables on Amy and see what she was thinking about the lifestyle, but she didn't give me much to go on. I'd push her more later.

The rest of the day went by in a blur, and I couldn't wait to curl up in bed with James and watch a little television. James seemed to have other plans, though. He took the remote from my hand and turned to sit cross-legged facing me.

"I've been thinking." His face was serious, so I just nodded to allow him to continue. He took my hands and smiled. "Things have been really great lately. Don't get me wrong, we've always had a terrific relationship, but recently it's been... better in some ways. If you would've asked me weeks ago if that was possible, I would've said no way. We were in our routine, and we were content.

"Anyway, going to these parties has been thrilling and something fresh. Although it's had an impact on our sex life in a *very* positive way." He swallowed hard before continuing, "I guess what I'm trying to say is that I'm not really interested in opening our bedroom to another couple. At least, not right now. I'm really glad we went to the hotel and that you've opened my eyes to something new and the toys have been great fun, too." He let out a huge breath and cupped my jaw in his palm. "Really, I just need you. You're more than enough, and I hope you feel the same way."

Relief washed over me at his words. "I'm so glad you said that I'd actually talked to Amy today, and she said a few things that got my mind going. I think the parties are exhilarating and add a little spice to our relationship, but I don't think I'd be comfortable with taking it any further than what we have. I never felt like our relationship was lacking, but I feel like we've reached a place that's fresh and new feeling—I love that."

"Me too, baby." He cradled my face in both hands and kissed me. It started off sweet and slow but quickly turned frantic. "I love you." He panted between kisses. "I need you."

Epilogue

Fifth Wheel

"Mama!" Jane shouted at me for the third time. I'd be trying to have a conversation with Amy, and she wouldn't stop interrupting me.

I leaned over so that I was eye to eye with her. "Jane, sweetie, you need to wait until mommy is done. What do you need?"

She patted my stomach a couple times. "Baby."

I tried to keep a poker face as Amy chuckled behind me. "No, sweetie, no baby."

Her angelic little face fell, and tears welled in her eyes.

I pulled her into my arms. "Don't cry, baby

girl." My heart broke for her, she was too young to understand.

"What happened?" My husband's voice was laced with concern.

Amy took it upon herself to fill him in. "She wants a baby."

James was wide-eyed when I looked up. "You do?"

"No, not me, Jane. She's upset that I am not having a baby."

"Aw, come here." He crouched down, and Jane went straight to him. He picked her up, soothing her. Within seconds she was squirming out of his arms and running back to play.

Amy found this humorous, I did not. "Guess you two better get to trying for another."

"Yeah, not happening," I blurted.

James looked down at me, surprise written all over his face.

"Looks like you two have some talking to do, so I'll leave you to it." Amy backed out of the room.

"You don't want any more kids?" His eyes crinkled at the sides.

"I mean, we haven't really talked about it, I —" I didn't know what to say. It's not like I had decided one hundred percent that I didn't want another child, but I liked how things were.

"I always thought we would have more."

I wrapped my arms around his waist. "I'm not saying it's completely off the table. I like the way things are right now, and I'm not looking to change that."

"Baby, I love how things are, too. I know another baby would change things some but not within our relationship. We would just be a little busier and have more little footsteps running around."

All I kept thinking was that we'd be right back to Sunday sex, and that was not an option for me.

"I know it's been a while since we talked about this, and last time we spoke, we wanted four. What's changed?"

I looked down, feeling selfish all of a sudden. I'd always wanted four kids, he's right, but I love the newfound intimacy we have now.

"Baby, look at me."

I looked up at him, and a tear slipped out.

"Clarissa, why are you crying?" He wiped his thumb across my cheek.

I blew out a breath. "I don't want to go back

to Sunday sex." My eyes averted his as I waited for his response.

"Is that it?"

I nodded.

"Baby, we're *never* going back to Sunday sex. *Ever*."

"How can you be so sure? We got stuck in our routine after Jane and—"

"I love the way things are between us and the excitement we have now in our love life. That's not going to change." He kissed me softly.

"You sound so sure of yourself."

His confidence needed to rub off on me.

"You'll get there." He kissed me again. "We're in no rush, so think about it. I'm positive you'll catch up to where I am."

<hr>

I rinsed out my mouth as I leaned over the sink and stared at myself in the mirror. "This can't be happening."

I'd felt like garbage for the last week and was finally going to the doctor today. I knew what it was but was in complete denial. After talking with James a few weeks ago about having more kids, I still wasn't entirely on board. I loved my kids to death, and I knew I had wanted more. However, I was content. And this time, it wasn't because of how monotonous it was. It was because I loved how exciting things were. I never knew when or how or where sex would happen, and I loved that. And I didn't want it to change.

I hadn't told James about my appointment, so when he called as I walked into the office, I silenced my phone and sent him a quick text telling him I would call him in a few.

"Clarissa, how are things?" Dr. Nina Lily was a great friend. We had gone to high school together. "You ready for this?" She knew I wasn't; I had called her freaking out.

"Absolutely not."

Thank God she had an in-house lab, so she could get me the results fast, not that I needed them. I'd been down this road a couple times; I was positive I was pregnant.

After they drew my blood, I sat there for a moment before Nina came back in. "I've let them know to rush this for me. Let's go grab some lunch. They'll call me when it's ready."

I'd picked at my food, not eating much. Every time her phone rang, my heart skipped a beat.

This time she looked at me before answering, I knew it was the lab. When she hung up, she set the phone down slowly.

"Holy shit, spit it out." I couldn't take it anymore.

"Congratulations," she said through her teeth.

I rolled my eyes. "My husband did this on purpose; I tell you, he tampered with my birth control. We literally had a conversation about having more kids a few weeks back, and I told him I wasn't ready." I dropped my head into my hands. I wasn't sure whether to laugh or cry.

"A few weeks ago?"

I looked up. "Yes. I'm just not ready yet."

"Well, if it makes you feel any better, this happened before that."

My eyes went wide. "Wait, what?"

"You're about ten weeks along based on your HCG levels."

"I'm what?" My voice was a little too loud for the quiet restaurant.

"Calm down, Riss." She reached her hand across and covered mine.

"I'm sorry, I guess it is what it is. I'm glad to

know it wasn't James's fault, though. He would be in big trouble."

Nina snickered. "It'll all work out; I truly believe things happen for a reason. I know right now it doesn't seem like the best plan, but have faith. You have two healthy kids and a man who adores you, and now you're being blessed with another child."

I took a few deep breaths. She was right. It wasn't the end of the world. Things could be much worse. It would take some time to get used to the fact that I was really having another baby, but it would be okay.

I squeezed her hand. "Thanks, Nina."

I didn't want to go home just yet, and since Jane was at my in-laws' house, I figured I would walk around the downtown shops. I found myself wandering into Snugglebugz without even thinking. The store had everything baby. I took my time, looking at all the adorable items, trying to get that excited feeling I always had when I was expecting. It didn't come. I felt like a horrible person for not being happy.

By the time I picked up Jane and got Lucas from the bus stop, my nerves were shot. How was

I going to tell James, and how would he react to my despondency?

I waited until after the kids went to bed to break the news to him. He'd asked me several times if I was okay, but I just blew it off like I had a headache. I wasn't sure he'd bought it, but he finally dropped it.

We brushed our teeth side by side before climbing into bed, and he pulled me back into him. "Baby, what's wrong?"

I finally let the tears I'd been keeping in all day fall.

James sat up and pulled me into his lap. "Talk to me, Riss. You're scaring me."

I shut down my pity party and pulled myself out of his lap to sit in front of him. I took a deep breath to calm myself and then looked up at him through blurry, tear-filled eyes. "I'm pregnant."

His concerned face morphed into one of pure joy, and it killed me that I didn't share in his happiness. "Oh my God, that's...wait, why are you crying? Is everything okay with the baby?"

I nodded my head, and his eyes went wide, completely misunderstanding me. "As far as I know, everything is all right. But *I'm* not all right.

I'm not ready for this, James. We discussed this, and I knew I wasn't ready."

"Baby." He leaned forward and kissed me breathless before pulling back only slightly. "I know you've got apprehensions about this, but trust me when I tell you, you have *nothing* to worry about."

"I—"

He didn't allow me to continue as he took my mouth with his, pushing me backward to lie on the bed. "No more talking." He kissed his way down my neck, and I was glad for the distraction.

He removed my pajamas and his quickly and then sat back on his haunches. "Turn over." His voice was hoarse and sexy as hell.

I loved it when he told me what to do in bed. I instantly obeyed and turned onto my stomach, keeping my ass in the air. He hummed his satisfaction as his hand softly rubbed circles on my backside before his hand lifted and came down hard.

A moan escaped my throat, and his hand came down again. He rand his fingers through my folds. "You like that, Clarissa?"

I nodded, unable to speak. I felt the bed shift

before he rubbed his head through my juices and then pushed forward to the hilt.

I cried out the moment he bottomed out and stilled. He gripped my hair, pulling me up to him. His teeth nibbled on my neck. His breath sending chills down my spine as he whispered in my ear. "This." He thrust forward. "Is." And again. "Never." And again. "Ending." His movements were hard and precise, showing rather than telling me that there was nothing to fear.

Before I could speak, he began a punishing rhythm. He kept hold of my hair and brought his hand down to circle my clit. I was so close to coming, but he wasn't going to let me just yet. He slowed his pace, rotating his hips ever so slightly, driving me crazy.

"I'm going to spend the next nine months showing you that no matter what, this isn't going to change. I've gotten a taste of this new life we have in the bedroom, and I'm never letting it go. So, whether you're nine months pregnant or we have ten kids, we will make time to fuck"—he reached up and pinched my nipped hard—"and make love and everything in between. I'm not done exploring everything there is with you, and

I won't be even if I had twenty lifetimes with you." He nipped my neck. "I love you."

"I love you, too."

He let me go and gripped my hips before he began his demanding assault again. This time he didn't let up and pushed us both over the edge. We collapsed on the bed, and he pulled me in close.

"My legs feel like jelly."

"Well, there's a lot more where that came from, and as I said, we will be doing that for the next nine months and beyond. No Sunday sex." He chuckled against my neck.

"Oh, I guess I forgot to mention. You actually only have six and a half months to show me that this isn't going to end."

He pulled my shoulder toward him and got up on his elbows to look into my eyes. "What do you mean?"

"I'm apparently ten weeks along. I guess our daughter is a little bit of a clairvoyant." I shrugged.

"Wow! Well, that means I need to work twice as hard." I felt his dick twitch against my leg, and my eyes went wide.

"Round two?" He cocked a brow.

Hell yeah, I was ready for round two and anything else that life threw at us. With this man at my side, I could conquer anything, even another baby.

The End

Don't miss out on news from

Kristie Leigh

Scan here to sign up

Acknowledgments

I started writing *A Side He'd Never Seen* in 2018 and had a lot going on at the time, so I put my laptop down and didn't write for quite some time. It took me a while to pick it back up again but I'm glad I did.

Thanks to my bestie and Jessi for encouraging me to push through and finish this one and a few other projects that were put on the back burner.

With love and gratitude,

Kristie Leigh
xoxo

Kristie Leigh is a fiery redhead and USA Today Bestselling Author who fell in love with small-town life long before she ever experienced it. Growing up, she dreamed of quiet streets, friendly neighbors, and the kind of close-knit community that feels like home. Now, she's living that dream in a rural Alabama town with her high school sweetheart and their three kids.

Her passion for small-town romance comes alive in her stories, where back roads and burning hearts lead to love, second chances, and the kind of happily-ever-afters that stay with you long after the last page.

Discover more about

Kristie Leigh

www.ingramcontent.com/pod-product-compliance
Lightning Source LLC
Chambersburg PA
CBHW071746150726
47998CB00005B/1823